ADVENTURE MURDER & MAYHEM

Bob Nothnagel

This book is a work of fiction. Names, characters, businesses, organizations, places, events, and incidences are the product of the author's imagination or are used fictionally. Any resemblance to actual persons, living or dead, or locales is entirely coincidental.

Tales of Adventure, Murder, and Mayhem

ISBN: 9798825455969

To my dear wife, Teresa, who keeps my kayak afloat and pointed in the right direction, who encourages me, and loves me for who I am. I couldn't have done this without you. You're the reason for Your Song.

Acknowledgments

It takes a village to raise a child. I'd like to thank members of the Group 5 writing group of the Hamilton Mountain Writers Guild, including James, Eric, Karel, Emilia, Ellesen, Christy, Sarah Mae, and Katie. Your insight has improved my writing and made me better. I'd also like to thank Darlene Andrus for crossing my T's and dotting my I's. Thanks to Mom and Dad for letting me roam through the woods and farmer's fields of Alliston as a child, untethered, allowing my imagination to grow. And a final thanks to my wife for allowing me to click away on the keyboard.

Contents

IT WAS THE WINTER OF '69

This is a true story.

"Twelve-year-olds can't go to the ice rink unsupervised. One of us has to be with them," my wife insisted.

"They're old enough to babysit, but they can't look after themselves?" I didn't get it.

"That's not the point. What would our kids think if we let the grandkids go by themselves?"

"I know. I know. Give me half an hour and I'll take them." I leaned back in my chair and glanced out the frosty window. A light sprinkle of snow fell, settling on the white backyard. I stared for some time, wondering why things had to be so complicated. Memories flooded my mind.

It was 1969. Man had walked on the moon. Trudeau was in office. The Beatles performed their last public appearance from the top of Apple Records. Woodstock attracted more than 300,000 rock and roll fans. Closer to home, we still ordered from Sears through a small catalogue storefront. Alliston had a Dairy Queen, two grocery stores, several independent shops, and a Canadian Tire the size of my current condo, all on the main drag.

I turned thirteen that year, along with most of my friends. Life was simpler back then. A big event for me was the monthly drive into Barrie to the Woolworths Mall, a ten-store extravaganza. There were no organized sports for kids. We created our own outdoor entertainment and kept ourselves busy. Parents never worried when their kids went to the park by themselves or took off for the day.

It was Christmas break and Gord, Barry, Jim, Tom, Bruce, Randy, and I wanted to do something exciting, so we planned to go winter camping by ourselves. A good location was the property the scouts used out on the Fifth line beside the Nottawasaga River. On the property was a structure with a corrugated tin roof, about forty feet long, and twenty wide. One end and some of the sides were walled with corrugated tin. It would provide a little protection from the weather. Inside was a large wood-burning oven where we could cook our meals and melt snow for water. I'd been there a lot with the scouts.

With our accommodations accounted for we composed a list of food. Peanut butter for sure, some bread, Lipton's chicken noodle soup, Nestles hot chocolate mix, and pork and beans. Our parents would probably want us to take some vegetables, but Tom had just learned beans were a vegetable, so we were good. Bruce figured we should take some red licorice, so we added that, as well.

Next came our equipment. We all had sleeping bags, snowsuits, and boots. We thought if we could borrow one of the troop boxes from scouts it would help. Our troop box was about four feet long, two wide, and three feet high. Inside were axes, saws, Coleman stoves and lanterns, and a bunch of other equipment we could use.

We wanted to do this all on our own and decided to walk the five miles to the campsite. We were a bit cocky and wanted to go cross country through the farmer's fields to get there. All of us had toboggans and we decided to load the troop box on one and our personal kit on the others.

We were almost set to go but needed to get our parent's permission. We used the standard procedure for getting permission in those days. Each of us said the other parents were letting their kids go so "you just haaave to let me go". Phone calls were exchanged and there were some tense moments, but everyone was allowed to go. There were concerns about us getting there and staying for several nights, but it was agreed that a parent would drive out each day to see how we were doing. We accepted, not that we had a choice, and would start our journey on the 27th of December.

It was only the 22nd and I think I was more excited about the camping than I was about Christmas day. Each of the guys chipped in five dollars, actually from their parents, and my Mom and I went to the IGA to purchase food for the trip, from a parentally modified list, although some of the good stuff remained.

I packed the clothes I figured I needed, then my Mom went through it and added Mom stuff, like underwear and, can you believe it, soap and a washcloth. I protested, but I got *the look*, you know the one, and gave in.

Christmas came and went, and the big day arrived. We agreed to leave by nine o'clock down at the end of William Street near Gord's house. Randy lived on the other side of town and his dad drove him over around eight-thirty. The others started poking their heads out their doors and I said goodbye to Mom. The troop box was at Gord's and we soon had that strapped to one of the toboggans. Our food was inside so we had two guys pulling and one pushing the box. Three other toboggans held all our other kit. Without much fanfare, we left the street and headed straight east, cross-country.

I'd like to say there were three feet of snow and we forged a dangerous trail toward our objective, but that would be fibbing a little. I can't say for sure how deep the snow was, but when I was breaking trail, it was above my knees. We all took turns breaking trail, pulling toboggans, and pushing. Everything was going great, and we were having a blast. Those of us not pulling laden toboggans began firing snowballs at the rest. That prompted counterattacks and full out snowball fights, the result never truly decided. The sun was shining, the wind was not too fierce, and the temperature manageable. It was going well.

Then we came to the first fence.

We looked for a gate to open, but that was not going to work with the amount of snow we had. We tried, but the bottom six inches was crusty snow and ice, freezing the gate shut. So, after some deliberation and another snowball fight, we decided to lay the empty toboggans on the fence upside down on both sides and form a kind of ramp up and down. The toboggans with our gear on it were not too much trouble to get over, but the troop box was a different story. We shoved and pulled but the angle was too steep. After a while, we unpacked the box and got it over, repacked, and took a short break.

I had no idea at the time about acreage and farmer's fields, but as I look back on it now, the fields must have been set up in ten acre lots. It was a demoralizing sight when we came across our next fence. Unpack, repack and carry on to the next fence. We crossed three fences in total, and it was exhausting and ate into our fun.

We were overjoyed to spot what was then Concession 2, now called Boyne Street. Three-quarters of a mile done, four more to go. We left the toboggans by the side of the road and played a bit of Shoot and Fall. I'm not even sure if that is its real name. You know the game I'm talking about though, where one of your buddies is the shooter and whoever does the best "death" fall wins and becomes the shooter. We were doing super dives into the ditch, it was about eight feet deep with drifted snow. Randy and Bruce were the best. One time Bruce dove off the fence post headfirst and went in up to his knees. We tried to yank him out and tore his boots off. One of us stuffed snow in them, I can't remember who, while the others tried to get him unstuck. He was mad at us for stuffing his boots, but we declared him the overall winner and that calmed him down.

Tom got us focused again by declaring it was noon. We sat and had some peanut butter sandwiches and realized that at this pace, three hours to do three-quarters of a mile, we would take another twelve hours to get to the campsite. As much as we hated to admit it, going cross-country was not going to work, so we decided to go north to the Fifth Side Road, east across to the Fifth Concession, then south to the campsite, adding two more miles, but making progress much easier. We justified it by convincing ourselves we didn't want to break any farmer's fence. With that lame excuse, we ventured north along Concession 2 with six more miles to travel.

***

Not much happened along the way except a couple of snowball fights and a few stops. There was a brisk wind and we had to hunker down behind some trees to avoid the chill. It was a welcome relief to reach the Fifth and head south, putting the wind at our backs. It was an even greater relief to be on the final descent to the bridge-crossing with the pavilion in sight.

We must have made good time because there was still some daylight left and we had time to get settled in. There was a small pile of wood beside the stove, but we needed more. Tom grabbed an ax and went to chop up some deadwood. Randy and Bruce took some toboggans and rounded up smaller scrub and branches. The rest of us laid out the pallets that were stacked inside the enclosure, unpacked the food, and started a fire in the large wood-burning oven. We set out the sleeping bags and blankets, did a little repositioning, and then collected some rocks to make the second fire location. It was positioned in the center of the structure so that our sleeping bags were between it and the oven. We piled the wood on the opposite side of the fire so some of the heat would reflect back. One of our toboggans was metal and we set it up there too. An area for our kybo was established before dark and we were ready for the night. Someone's parents had remembered to pack some toilet paper, much to our relief.

When the others returned, we began supper. Randy became our cook as his father was an outfitter and he had the most experience, not that he needed much to warm up the pork and beans. We had a large pot which was filled with snow to melt for water. Most of us had canteens, you know, the round ones that are somewhat flat with a plastic screw lid chained to it. With both fires going it was comfortable, if not warm. We were able to take off our boots and dry them by the fire and hang up our coats, mitts, and snowsuits. Long-johns, socks, and running shoes were sufficient for moving around in the pavilion as we mostly hung around the fires. Hot chocolate and tea warmed us up and we talked about the day, joked about who had the goofiest dives, who did the least amount of work, school, and a bunch of other topics I won't bore you with. Randy had the best stories about his dad while he was outfitting. I think we prolonged our talks to avoid climbing into our cold sleeping bags, but eventually, drowsiness overcame us. After stoking the fires one last time we poured boiling water in our canteens and took them to bed to help keep us warm. I think the cold sleeping bags woke us up a bit and we talked some more but eventually, we drifted off.

The next morning, we woke up shivering. We were supposed to have taken turns stoking the fire during the night, but that never happened. A deep cold had settled in overnight and the temperature had plummeted. I think we all realized we had full bladders at the same time and made a mad dash to the kybo. After we got back it took a long time getting the fire going because our hands were shaking so badly. Luckily there were still embers in the wood stove, and we stoked it with shavings and small twigs. When it was blazing again, we lit a good-sized-stick on fire and transferred it to the other fireplace and slowly built it up too. We were going through our wood at an alarming rate so after some pork and beans we all headed out to collect firewood. The exercise warmed us up and we worked the morning gathering brush and logs. We had some soup for lunch and tried thawing some licorice for a snack.

In the afternoon we went over to a farmer's field to the south-east where there was a big hill leading down to the river. We spent the rest of the day tobogganing and building snow forts, with many a snowball fight thrown in. Exhausted, we headed back to the camp and fried up some wieners. Hot chocolate, tea, and a warm fire re-energized us for more storytelling.

One of our parents came out after dark, though I don't remember which one, but I think it was Barry's dad, to check on us. We claimed we were okay, and he stayed for a bit, I think more to check the place out than to hang out with us. After a while, he left, and I'm sure reported to all the other parents. We settled in for the night, the end of day two of our excursion, with more banter and promises of stoking the fire during the night, but as you might have guessed, that never happened.

Day three morning went similar to day two, waking up frozen, rushing to the kybo, fumbling with the fires, and eating some more beans. Our wood supply was good, but we still went out in the morning to gather some. We decided to play a little Blackbeard while we were out there. If you haven't played Blackbeard before, it's a savage game where you break off the ends of sticks against a tree, baseball style, and try to hit your opponent.

We spent more time in the afternoon tobogganing and had some snowball fights. The temperature dropped so we headed back to the warmth of the fires early. We got a good blaze going and hung up our snowsuits and boots. Our clothes were wet and cold, so we were anxious to get them dried. The hot chocolate was running low, so we drank tea and cooked up some ravioli for an afternoon snack.

Supper came and we had more pork and beans. We had just brewed another kettle of tea when Randy's dad showed up. He brought his snow machine on the back of his truck and offered us rides. We scrambled to get dressed and took turns racing up and down Concession 5, trying to go faster than the last guy. We were probably not going too fast as most of us were inexperienced drivers, but even at thirty miles an hour, it was exhilarating. It was getting late, and we wrapped up the driving and loaded the machine in the back of the truck and then Randy's dad came to inspect our campsite.

He eyed it over pretty well and we waited anxiously for his critique. His only comment, although he probably had many thoughts he didn't share, was to exact a promise from us to keep a fire watch at night. This was for two reasons: One for safety. At any time, a log could explode and a shower of sparks cover us. The second was that the temperature would be dropping very low that night and the fires needed to remain stoked. He also recommended we wear our toques to bed to help keep us warmer. With that sage advice and a look that froze us more than the weather, we promised to keep a fire watch from now on. So, we settled in for the night and took turns watching the fire for an hour and a half each.

Day four started much colder. At least the fires were going when we woke up and snuggled close for warmth. We were hanging around the pavilion longer during the morning. I think we were getting tired of the routine, of being cold and wet all the time, and of being downright exhausted. None of us would admit it to any of the others, but I believe we were all feeling the same way. We decided we needed a "maintenance" day, clean up around the camp, dry out wet clothes, and gather more firewood.

Just before noon, Gord complained of a stomachache. He was shivering and had a fever. We got him over to the cookstove to warm up and gave him some soup. Then he started ralphing. He laid a huge one all over the top of the stove. It looked like a huge bean omelet and smelt really bad. Luckily, he missed the soup but ralphed a few more times. We tried some crackers, but he couldn't keep them down, either. We had a cold cloth on his forehead and tried rubbing his belly, but after watching him shiver and ralph some more, we figured he may need to see a doctor or something. He said he was fine, but after he started dry-heaving Tom and I went to the farm close by and asked if we could use the phone. We called his parents and explained the situation. They said they would be out right away so we headed back to the camp after thanking the farmer.

When Gord's Mom and Dad arrived they took one look at him and put him into the car. They headed off and we found out later they went straight to the hospital where he was admitted for food poisoning and a fever of 105. That caused a series of phone calls and a visit by my Dad. He was the manager in the commissary on base and was responsible for its cleanliness. He checked around the camp for any signs of poor hygiene. I thought we had done a pretty good job of washing pots and dishes and not melting any yellow snow. When he poured out the tea to have a drink was when he spotted the problem.

At this time I must tell you about our tea. My Mom had packed a kettle and a bunch of tea bags so we could drink it to keep warm. None of us knew how to make tea, my granny had it often enough, but she had a teapot. We didn't have one of those so we just filled the kettle with water and stuffed a dozen bags in there. The water boiled for half an hour or so and we would pour it into our cups and drink it. When we went to make new tea we couldn't get the old bags out, so we just shoved some more in there. After a while, we got less and less water in the kettle and more tea bags.

Apparently, we had never spotted the black stuff floating around in the tea or had chosen to ignore it. Either way, he figured that was the culprit. When he learned we were stuffing the tea bags in the kettle and leaving them there, he shook his head. We were supposed to stay another night, but my Dad put a stop to it and told us to pack up. He went back to Alliston and got a couple of other parents to help transport all our gear.

At the time we protested and whined about not completing our camping trip and that we wanted to walk back the next day and it wasn't fair, but to be honest, I don't think any of us could have walked back home. We were cold, wet, exhausted, and it wouldn't have been the same without Gord. We put up a good fight, but I think we all were secretly relieved when the cars showed up later that day. I was for sure. We certainly had everything packed and ready to go and scrambled into those cars. The heaters were on full blast and our complaining stopped as we told our stories in detail.

Over the next few days, a lot of time was spent washing clothes, hanging sleeping bags, and scrubbing pots and pans. I had to work extra hard on a certain red-handled kettle, fishing out black, moldy teabags and flushing out the interior. It finally passed my Mom's inspection. I have that same kettle today and still use it to boil water on camping trips. Although now I put the tea bags in my cup. Gord came home after a couple of days and we all got together over the next week or so to hash over our adventure. Why Gord was the only one to get sick, we could never figure out.

As I look back on our little trip, four days and three nights in the cold by ourselves, I wonder at a lost time. A time of no cell phones, no video games, a time where kids went out and organized their own fun, and looked after themselves. Certainly, no parent today would let their thirteen-year-old go winter camping out in the boonies. But that's just the way it was back in the winter of '69.

THE FARMER

Nothing unusual happens this far north in the Kingdom. Until today. It was mid-afternoon when I noticed the dust plumes far to the north. A half dozen riders, maybe eight. They looked to be in full gallop, approaching the farm. I pulled back the reins on my plow horse. Something was up. I unhitched the plow and urged Benny toward the barn. He was tired but we needed to get back to the safety of the farmhouse.

I looked around at the fruits of my labour. Fields of corn and barley spread out before me. I'd been working this land for fifteen years now, a gift from the King, for services rendered to the realm. Sometimes I wondered if it was an honor or a curse. At least I got top prices for my crops.

I led Benny to the water trough in the shade of the barn. There was still feed in the manger to keep him happy. I dunked my head in the cool water, holding it under for several seconds, coming up only after I could hold my breath no more. The water drained off my head and down my shirt, relieving the heat of the day. Looking to the north, I noticed the riders were almost here.

I hurried over to the house to grab my crossbow, in case of trouble. I also prepared the kettle for coffee and dug out some scones in case there was no trouble. They were harder than rocks and tasted like donkey shit. I may be able to work the land, and other things, but I could not bake worth a hill of beans. My wife had passed on twelve years ago, and I had been losing weight ever since.

The riders pulled up to the house and dismounted. Seven, as I figured. My body may be fading, but my eyes were still good. They had full plate mail armour and etched on their breast a sigil of an ax splitting the skull of an Ogre. Orez Riders. I put the crossbow down and stepped outside. They'd seen recent battle too, from the blood on their armour. The Orez Riders had been formed generations ago when humans first settled in the area. The King had commissioned the group and given them their own sigil. Their sole responsibility was to rid the Kingdom of raiding Ogres, which came from the Orez Forest north of here.

"We shall need provisions and shelter for the night," called out the leader. "And a fresh horse for my rider to fetch reinforcements."

He had the standard sigil emblazoned on his armour. As well, above the right breast, the Fist of Deemore with a 15 beneath it, meaning he was the commander, the fifteenth. I thought it a bit odd for the commander of the Orez Riders to be accompanied by so few warriors.

"You are most welcome to stay, my Lord, although the accommodations are meager, and the food more so. My fastest horse, which is slow enough I'm afraid, is in the third stall of the barn. If it pleases you, your rider may ready the nag faster than myself. My Lord, there are not many in your escort. Was there trouble?" He was certainly no Lord. Commanders of the Orez Riders are not Lords. They are assigned their command by the King. But it did no harm to call him so.

He looked at one of his men. "Rogist, prepare the horse and ride for reinforcements. Gather them all. There should be three hundred plus. We'll need them all for a counterattack." He glanced around at the others. "The rest of you, see to the horses and find someplace to bed down in the barn. At dusk, we will start a watch. But first, get this cursed armour off me." After his armour was removed, he turned to me. "Now, to your inquiry. We were ambushed by a band of Ogres outflanking us."

I pondered the commander's words, as his rider galloped off for the reinforcements and the others looked after their horses.

"Would you care to join me for some refreshments?" I gestured to the porch.

"Yes, I am dry from all this riding. Your lands are dusty and barren. What have you got?"

"There is coffee and Sweetwater. I'm afraid that is all I have, my Lord."

"Sweetwater will do." You can sit for a bit, but then you must prepare our supper." answered the commander.

I gathered the refreshments and scones and sat beside him, a small table between us. With his helmet off I now recognized his face. I had come across him before. Long ago. He seemed not to recognize me. "There must have been many Ogres," I stated.

"There *were* many. We fought well, but they overtook us, and we had to retreat."

"How many do you think?" I probed further.

"My scouts underestimated their numbers. Their incompetence was rewarded with death." He looked at me. "Tactics do not concern one such as you. We will talk no more of this. I gladly accept the offer of your bed. If you have no other, you may bed with the rest in the barn."

I thought this arrogant bugger a bit too full of himself. He had been like that back in the day and even more so, now. Command sometimes makes people large in the head. However, with that larger head does not come additional wisdom. That was proven by his loss of men in the field. That was too bad for them. The commander had made a mistake and blamed his scouts. I could say nothing though. It would do no good. When he spoke no more, I got up and went to prepare dinner.

The meal came and went without incident. The soldiers were cordial, if not friendly, and the conversation was limited. The brooding commander's brooding demeanour spilled over the room, nullifying any attempt at hospitality. I'm sure their thoughts were with their fallen comrades and the battle just lost. Mine was with how to get through this inconvenience the best way possible. A day lost in the fields. Likely tomorrow too. At least Benny would get a rest. Not me though. They would want a full breakfast and possibly lunch. I would need to travel to Grimshaw's for more supplies after that. There would not be enough for tomorrow's supper. I was also concerned about the Ogres.

After supper, I cleaned up by myself. There was no offer of help. The men went about their business in the barn. The commander sat at the table, looking at maps and mumbling to himself. I worked around him gathering plates and cups. He said not a word to me, and I found that for the best. He would not want to hear what I had to say. I finished tidying and looked at the commander.

"Will there be anything else?" I had dropped the Lord. He didn't deserve it.

"No. That's it. You are dismissed."

Dismissed. From my own house. For a gold piece, I'd slit this incompetent ass' throat. But then where would that leave me? In a stockade somewhere, or dead. I might be able to sneak in and kill the other five, but the reinforcements would be here tomorrow. Either way, I would be done. Besides, I knew full well the men were not to blame for their leader.

I gathered an extra wool blanket, and a pitcher of Sweetwater, bade my farewell to the arrogant bastard, and walked over to the large oak tree. It was several hundred yards from the house. I chose to be here tonight instead of in the barn. My wife's grave lay near it. Poor Carley. The Pox took her one cold winter day. She fought hard and almost came out of it, but in the end, it was for naught. I missed her so. She was my rock, the glue that held the farm together. I wanted to be close to her tonight. She would give me comfort.

Before I slept for the night, I checked on Benny. The men were settling in. Some were repairing tack, others sharpening blades. A rotating guard was set up. I heard a couple talking.

"He buggered us all, I say."

"Yep, letting them brutes flank us like that."

"The scouts told him, but he wouldn't listen."

"No reserve force."

"Poor at tactics. Fifteen years at command, and still hasn't learned."

"Ah, makes me want to puke."

Soldiers always have an opinion. Always questioning their leaders. In this case, I thought them to be right. It would not be good to have them know I heard them. I slipped away and bade the others a good night and walked back to the oak tree. The ground was hard here, so I scooped out a hip hollow, and settled down for the night. Carley was near, giving me comfort. I rustled deeper into my wool blanket and settled in for the night. Tomorrow the reinforcements would come, and I would be rid of these pests. I could get on with my life, for what it was worth.

***

I heard the horn blow as the moon was coming up on the horizon. I was confused at first, to where I was, and what the horn meant. The fogginess of sleep slipped away, and I began to remember the commander and his men. The horn could only mean one thing. An attack!

There were about fifty of the large brutes trampling across the fields. The low moon cast eerie long shadows, enlarging the already huge monsters. Ogres! The Orez Riders came running out of the barn in various states of attire. They fared well, I'll give them that, killing about a third of the Ogres, but in the end were overrun. The Lord Commander was the second last to go down. I cringed as I watched the Ogres ravage the barn, destroying all the livestock. I listened in horror as the animals screamed. Most were in pens or chained to posts. Poor Benny.

They finished their destruction and ambled away to the north. Back to their forest. For the most part, they left the house alone. I was lucky to be far enough away, and they paid no notice. I dared not check anything in the dark in case some beasts were still lingering.

This was strange, new behavior from the Ogres. I had never seen them travel this far and attack the farmsteads. Normally they just fed near their forest. Was this some sort of revenge, if they were even capable of that thought? Had they gained confidence with their recent victory? I pondered these and many other thoughts well into the night as sleep eluded me.

It was after dawn when I felt safe enough to get up, achy from staying the night outside. The oak tree had protected me from most of the evening moisture, but the dampness still seeped into my tired bones. A light, misty fog hung over the land, partially obscuring the damage. Trudging over to the barn, I surveyed the mess that was left. As I suspected; everything dead. The smell of blood and gore overcame me. Half-eaten carcasses strewn about. There was Benny. I only knew it was him from the colour of his fur. I turned my back to him. My body tensed as I felt the pounding in my temples. I could not move. My jaw worked, grinding my teeth and I sweat profusely.

"Enough!" I screamed. "When will this end?"

It would take all my efforts to clean this up. I wasn't sure I even wanted to. Clean all this, just to start over again. Just to have the privilege to work hard for the rest of my life. It didn't need to be. I had a sturdy rope on that peg over there. A nice beam over there. I could join my Carley. We could be together again. It would be so nice.

I grabbed the rope and tossed it over the beam. It was long enough. I was about to climb up the ladder when I heard a dull sound outside, then a slight tremor at my feet. I put my ear to the ground. Horses.

I shook my head and walked out of the barn. The fog had lifted. I noticed the huge plume of dust, rising from the south, this time. The reinforcements were coming, hundreds, by the look of it. My spirits were lifted. That stubborn determination I've had all my life stiffened my backbone. I raised my head. It would not end like this.

I made my way into the home I'd lived in for fifteen years. I sat down at the kitchen table. There were many things to do. I would need help to rebuild the damaged barn. I could rely on Dannik from the next farm for that. The livestock would need replacing. I knew how to arrange that. They will owe me many things in the next few weeks. But, I thought, first things, first.

I got up and dragged the kitchen table to the side. There, covered in years of dust was a steel ring embedded in the floor. I brushed the dust and dirt away and grabbed the ring. Straining my muscles, the joints creaking loudly, I lifted the trap door to the root cellar. Well, it may have been a root cellar when Carley was alive, but I had not been down here in years. I mentioned I can't cook very well. I can't prepare vegetables for storage either.

I ambled down the stairs. They were old and rickety, similar to me. There was no banister to steady myself, so I took my time. My boots seemed heavy, and my shoulders stooped as I approached the chest in the far corner. I lifted the lid and peered inside. I blew the dust off the contents and kneeled there, staring. The sigil of the Orez Riders was emblazoned on a set of full plate mail. Although nicked and dented from many battles, it was still visible. My eyes moved to the right breast. Above it was the Fist of Deemore with the number 14 underneath.

I grabbed my mail and slowly dragged it upstairs. I knew the Orez Riders would need their old commander back now. The Gods had not favored the new one.

The King had not done well assigning him to the position.

VACCINE

Doctor Jennifer Branson followed the three other passengers into the first-class compartment of the Boeing 777.

"I can take that, Ms. Branson," the flight attendant offered.

"Thank you." Jennifer handed her coat, scarf, gloves, and hat to the thirtyish-year-old lady.

"Is Frankfurt your final stop?"

"No," Jennifer replied. "I'm continuing on to Geneva."

"Oh, how nice. Switzerland is beautiful in January."

"Yes, I've only ever seen it in the summer."

The flight attendant took her things and hung them up in a closet near the front. Jennifer could not help but wonder about the attendant and what was in store for her and others. The attendant stored the overnight bag in the compartment above. A thin briefcase remained with Jennifer. She settled into a soft lounge chair and arranged her belongings. She removed her laptop and opened it. On her desktop were two folders. She opened the first. It contained pages of research data on Covid-19, the various vaccines, and their side effects. The second contained results of genetic testing done in her lab over the last four months. She spent a lot of the flight going over the numbers.

Jennifer worked at the Center for Disease Control and Prevention. Although she had a doctorate in Virology and Epidemiology, her main interest and expertise was in gene studies. Her presentation to the WHO could shape health protocols for years to come.

The engines began spooling up.

The flight attendant came by. "We will be taking off shortly. Please fasten your seatbelt and watch the safety video. Supper will be served once we reach our cruising altitude. Will you be having the steak or pasta alfredo?"

"I think I'll try the steak, please."

"Of course. I'll bring the drink cart once we're airborne."

"I'll just have water for now, thanks."

Jennifer returned to her papers. The numbers were impressive. 2021 had been a whirlwind year. Initially slow, the vaccine rollout had increased after June. By the fall close to 87% of the United States were completely vaccinated; however, numerous variants triggered a fourth and fifth wave, higher infection rates and hospitalizations. Deaths had skyrocketed. The most alarming variant had been the B.1.1.787 which affected children and teens. Just over 19% of the infected had died from the variants in those age groups, a staggering 8 million in the U.S. Panic struck worldwide. Research into a booster vaccine began. It had rolled out in January of 2023. An executive order was signed, and vaccines were mandated in the United States. Most countries followed and a massive inoculation process followed. By July of that year 97% of the United States was fully vaccinated. The rest of the world was around 95%.

The seat vibrated as the engines roared and the plane raced down the runway. It lifted off and Jennifer watched the Atlanta skyline disappear in the distance. Soon the plane entered the clouds and she returned to her papers.

It was 2025 and things were getting back to normal. There were still pocket outbreaks, but lockdowns had been lifted, and the economy was returning to normal. Even the hotspots had settled down and hospitals there were at normal capacity. Governments were frantically trying to get their countries back to normal.

Jennifer closed her laptop. Geneticists from twelve other countries were attending the conference. Dr. Kay from Canada, Dr. Bennet from England and Dr. Brisbois from France were but a few she knew of. Along with them was a sociology and economics expert giving a lecture.

Her steak arrived and she ate slowly, enjoying the red wine that accompanied it. The hum of the plane and the late hour eventually caused her eyes to droop. She adjusted the seat and fell asleep.

She awoke to an announcement of breakfast and was soon enjoying a hearty eggs Benedict and coffee. The plane began descending as the dishes were cleared away. Forty-five minutes later she was walking down the concourse to her connecting flight. There was a two-hour wait, so she settled into a chair in the first-class lounge and opened a file on her laptop.

Currently, less than .1% of the world's population was not vaccinated. That was a huge success and a savior for stopping the spread of Covid-19, but there were other disturbing factors which were the topic of her speech tomorrow. She went over her notes once more, wondering what words she would use to convey the message.

***

The next morning Jennifer was seated on the side of the stage of the auditorium in the WHO headquarters. Alongside her were five other scientists from various fields and countries. The emcee was addressing the crowd.

"If you could all take your seats, we have several guest speakers making presentations today, all of which will have a profound impact on the world's health. We'll start with Dr. Branson." She looked at Jennifer. "Dr. Branson."

Jennifer took to the podium, her knees a little wobbly. "Good morning, ladies and gentlemen. I'm Dr. Branson from the CDC. I'm going to be talking about a specific side effect from the booster vaccine developed in late 2022 and administered in early 2023.

"Reports began filtering in December of 2023 and, when significant incidences occurred, my department was notified. We reached out to the various institutions and, by August 2024, had just over ten thousand cases reported. In every case of male recipients of the Covid -19 booster, the sperm count had no *Y* sperm cells. Something had eliminated the *Y* chromosome. Before I get into the problem let me explain some basic genetics.

"The *X* and *Y* chromosomes determine sex. Two *X* chromosomes make a female and an *XY* combination makes a male. Everyone here knows that. What you may not know is that over the last 160 million years the *Y* chromosome has lost 1,393 of its 1,438 original genes or roughly 97%. The Covid-19 booster destroyed the remaining genes.

"After extensive testing, we reached out to our colleagues in Europe to assist in the research. They have all confirmed our results with their cases.

In every one of the cases presented, in thirty-seven countries worldwide so far, the *Y* chromosome has disappeared."

There was mumbling amongst the audience of scientists.

"It has been determined with two hundred and fifty thousand cases that the booster vaccine has sped up the deterioration of the *Y* chromosome. We can extrapolate that to mean that 99.9% of the male population is unable to produce male offspring. In addition, we have determined that any female who has had the booster and has a male child with an unvaccinated male will still only have a one in four chance that the child can produce a *Y* chromosome. We have yet to determine whether that child will lose their capability to produce *Y* chromosome sperm later in life. Essentially we will have a female dominated population in one hundred years."

An outcry of alarm and speculation ran through the auditorium as opinions were voiced, solutions presented, and doomsday scenarios gone over.

The emcee walked up to the microphone holding up his hands. "Please. Please. Settle down. Dr. Branson, thank you for that presentation. We will now turn the mike over to Dr. Lansing, a professor of sociology." He motioned to a man waiting at the side. "Dr. Lansing."

A middle-aged man of medium height walked up to the podium. "Distinguished colleagues and guests. I wish I were up here to give better news but I'm afraid it will be quite sobering. I assure you that I am no alarmist, and I base my facts on some projection curves, but this is very real.

"My distinguished colleague set out the scenario of our future from a geneticist's viewpoint. I'm going to look at it from a sociological and geographical viewpoint, including infrastructure and survivability. Let's look at a standard one-million-person test case as an example.

"Out of those one million, approximately 927 of those did not receive the vaccine for various health reasons. The following numbers relate only to persons that did not receive the vaccine. There are 567 females of which 207 are of child rearing age. Out of the 360 males, only 227 are capable of producing viable sperm.

"Let's fast forward 20 years. By then, 107 males will have died off by natural causes, leaving 120 males from the original, plus a projected 200 new males capable of production for a total of 320.

"On the female side, 87 females will have died with a further 23 who will be incapable of having babies, leaving 97 from the original, plus a projected 210 new females capable of reproduction for a total of 307.

"At first, this looks like growth, but there are numerous factors to add to this formula. For instance, this is assuming a couple are both non-vacs and all are matched up. If only half of the remaining non-vacs were a couple, the numbers would be greatly reduced. It also assumes that an eligible female would be willing to have a child every three years. Another consideration is that the original reason these people did not get the vaccine is because of various health reasons. This could result in a high rate of death amongst the group.

"Other factors should be considered. After forty years, a lot of the population will have died off as well as the support personnel to maintain infrastructure. There will be replacements but not at a rate that will maintain the status quo. Electricity, water, natural gas, gas at the pumps, and hospitals will all eventually fail. We will revert to a mid-to-late 1800s standard. Harsh conditions will cause migrations to warmer climates. Most homes are ill-equipped to heat themselves in winter, having no wood fireplace or, at most, an inadequate one to heat the entire house.

"Food supply will be another problem, as well as medications. Anxiety will run rampant when the internet breaks down. Communication will be lost, and information unavailable. Society will then deteriorate, and chaos abound."

A hand shot up from the crowd.

"Yes, sir."

"Surely, we will survive, though. This is all alarming, but we can adapt. Set up breeding programs. Like the zoos. Ensure mankind survives."

Dr. Lansing motioned to Jennifer. "I'll let my distinguished colleague answer that."

Jennifer walked up to the mike. "We've taken a dangerous virus and used technology to develop a vaccine to combat the virus. We defeated it, but in so doing, sealed the fate of mankind. The facts do not lie. With the genetics information we have, and with Dr. Lansing's predictions factored in, it is my belief that mankind will be extinct within 200 years."

Jennifer was leaving the auditorium when Dr. Lansing approached her.

"Dr. Branson, would you be interested in attending a meeting tonight? There is a group of individuals wishing to hear from you about a solution to the situation."

"What group?" she asked. "I wasn't told of this."

"It's a think tank of world leaders trying to come up with a viable solution. It is most urgent that you attend."

"I suppose I could. When is it?"

"Tonight at 8:00. They will pick us up at 7:00."

"Seven. Why? Where is this meeting?"

"It is at the home of one of the interested parties. Outside the city a few kilometres."

"I suppose I can attend."

"Great. I'll meet you at your hotel lobby at five to. Thank you."

Jennifer watched her countryman walk to the auditorium bar and grab a drink. She hailed a cab and it dropped her off at her hotel. She was intrigued by this meeting and curious about who would be there. The hotel restaurant offered a great lobster brisque, but she declined the wine and stuck with water.

***

The limousine climbed the road up the mountainside toward an unknown destination. The driver had been courteous but quiet. Dr. Lansing engaged in idle chitchat. A large mansion appeared from around a bend, and they stopped by the main doors.

Inside, a butler took their coats and escorted them into a large study. Centred in the room stood a square table with ample room for the twenty or so individuals already seated. The walls, at least thirty feet high, contained four levels of books, accessed by a sliding ladder. Jennifer turned her attention to the persons seated. Everyone was well but casually dressed, and at an age range between forty and seventy. She recognized several of them. Two had designed and used their own rockets to go into space. If the others were as important, this represented a powerful world group.

A lady stood up.

"Welcome Dr. Branson, Dr. Lansing. Please have a seat." She motioned to the empty chairs. After they were seated, she addressed everyone.

"We are here tonight to see if we can come up with a solution to our current problem with this vaccine. Obviously, it will create many challenges as we move forward. Dr. Branson, as you can imagine, my colleagues and I represent some very powerful and influential groups throughout the world. It is our goal tonight to come up with a plan to maintain humanity, no matter how drastic the measures. We've asked you here for your input on genetic matters. Before you is a report composed by several of those present. We've all had the opportunity to read it except you, Dr Branson. Let me summarize.

"Dr. Lansing has identified that we have 20 years, possibly 30, before the damage is irreversible. Natural reproduction by area, finding viable mates, and sociological conditions will make it almost impossible to produce male offspring. We must have a solution before then, preferably in the next two years. Dr. Branson, I know great strides have been made in the production of sperm in the lab. Can you and a team of researchers perfect the process, ensuring the *Y* chromosome is present?"

"Yes, I'm sure we could, but it would be faster if several laboratories were researching."

"Out of the question for now," the lady announced. Jennifer sat back wondering where this was going.

"John," the lady addressed a man in his fifties. How are the patents coming?"

"My legal team has gone over all current patents pertaining to this subject. There are loopholes. If worded correctly, and with a specific procedure identified by Dr. Branson, we could have the exclusive patent to produce and sell the *Y* chromosome sperm in 187 counties. The remaining countries are irrelevant. They are too small or underdeveloped to be of consequence."

"Wait," Jennifer stood. "Patents. Selling. What about the survival of our race?"

An elderly gentleman cleared his throat and chuckled. "It's just like the scientists. My dear, of course we are interested in the human race." His voice and demeanor reminded her of Gandalf explaining the simplest of concepts to Frodo. "We need mankind around to sell our product to.

"Our main concern is making money."

A TRAIL IN THE WOODS

The powder blue Lexus ES 350 slowed to a crawl on Guelph Line just north of the 401.

"OMG, there it is." O squealed. "Number 9475, just like the app says." She sat in the passenger seat, smartphone in one hand, a Starbucks Grande, vanilla latte with soy in the other. Her dirty blonde hair was tied up in a loose bun. She wore a light gray Saint Laurent hoodie with matching sweatband. Givenchy Stretch Knit Leggings covered her lower limbs.

Zack glanced at her, smiling. "Let's do this." He turned the car into the skinny lane leading to the path they were walking today. According to the app, there was a small parking lot at the trailhead. "Hashtag adventure!" he exclaimed.

"Stop!" O yelled. "Look, isn't that gravel or something? I heard about that stuff on Facebook." She looked at Zack. "Does our warranty cover driving on that? Let me check." She placed her latte down and began searching her phone.

"We'll be fine. Remember, we vowed to be adventurous." He eased the car forward, cringing at the occasional ping of a flying pebble. Trees bracketed the single lane with bushes encroaching. A branch lightly grazed the car. O screamed. After fifty feet the lane opened up into a small parking lot. Zack let out his breath. “See, no problem.” He looked at her and nodded, running his hand through his Bumble and Bumble gelled hair.

“Wait.” She pointed. “There’s a Yaris parked here. Hashtag embarrassing. What do we do?”

“It’ll be okay. I’ll park as far away as I can so no one thinks we’re together.” He steered the car into the farthest parking spot from the Yaris, frequently glancing back at the car. Zack grabbed his latte as they both got out of the car. He wore an RW&Co slim fit knit blazer over a Jack’s Mannequin t-shirt. Duer No Sweat jogger pants covered his legs and Vessi Waterproofs were on his feet.

“I can’t believe we’re doing this,” O said as they walked to the trailhead sign. “An actual trail in the woods. Hashtag Zach and O, hashtag wild. Selfie time. Move in.” They shuffled into the frame, her arm fully extended, cell phone at the ready. After seven clicks they turned to start down the trail. O stopped in her tracks. “What. Is. That?”

Zack bent over, eyeing the ground. “I’m pretty sure it’s dirt.” He stood up, looking at O. “The trail is made of dirt. They want us to walk on this?” He brought his hands up to his face, covered his eyes, slowly drawing them down to his chin. “That’s it. I’m texting that app.” His thumbs flew about his phone. “They can’t do this to us. Where is the contact number? Oh, I’m sooo tweeting about this.”

“Me too. Wait! What about my Louis Vuittons? I’ll get them dirty. Hashtag downer.”

“There.” He stared at his phone. “Oh good, I’ve got 67 likes. I feel, like, a little better now. Do you think we could try this?”

“Look here. I’ve got 103 likes on Twitter and 17 already on Facebook. Te-Te says, ‘You go Girl.’ Zack, let’s do this. Hashtag BeBrave.”

The two started down the path, lattes in one hand, smartphones in the other. The path varied in width. Tall spruce trees, branches missing for some ten metres up, mingled with maple and an occasional birch. Smaller bushes filled in the brush underneath, guiding them down the hard-packed trail.

“Look, Zack. I’m videoing this so we can watch it through the phones. Uploading it to VidMov. All our friends will be envious...”

Zack screamed, jumping about, clawing at his face. “O. M. G. Look, O! I have cobwebs on my face.”

“Cobwebs?” She started thumbing her phone. “What are cobwebs?”

“Cobwebs! They’re from ticks. You can get Lyme disease from touching the cobwebs. It’s a horrible disease. I could get really sick and not be able to party. I might even lose my job.” He stood there shaking, his hands out in front of him. “I need a safe place — right, now!”

O looked around. “They don’t provide any. Oh wait, I have that app.” She thumbed her phone and soon soft whale music and trickling water flowed out its speaker. “There, how’s that? Oh no, Zack!” She grabbed his arms. “No. If you get sick and can’t work, we may lose the Lexus. We won’t be able to make the payments.”

“What? Hey, what about me?” He cocked his head, eyeing her. Then his mouth fell open. “Oooh, no, not the Lexus.”

“Don’t worry, I’m looking up cures right now. We have that first aid kit from Mountain Equipment Co-op, right.” O thumbed through her phone. Her face scrunched up as she read for several minutes. “Wait. You can’t get Lyme disease from cobwebs. And ticks don’t even make cobwebs. They hang in grasses. Here, I’ll Pushbullet you this Wiki article.”

Zack read for several minutes. A sheepish grin came over his face. “I guess I panicked over nothing. This is so like that movie, Arctic, survival and all that. Shall we continue?”

“Yeah, totally.” They began walking again. O laughed. “I wonder what some of the young kids nowadays would have done. They’re so sheltered.”

The path opened up a little as they continued their walk. They came to an open field with power lines stretching as far as they could see. It was humid but not uncomfortably so. A squirrel bounded by, ignoring them. At the other end of the clearing, pine trees dominated the forest, a thick bed of needles carpeting the open areas. It darkened as they entered, the forest canopy blocking out the sun.

“Whoa, look at this. It’s like a whole different path.”

They eased into a comfortable stride, their matching Adidas sweatpants rustling. Liv’s curls bounced as she shook her large head of hair. Zach’s white Metallica t-shirt showed the first signs of sweat. The squirrel watched them, perched on a stump. It chattered and scampered off. A strange static in the air caused the hair on Zach's arm to rise. He momentarily glanced over his shoulder.

"Hey, Zac-man, I told you this place was totally rad."

"It's an adventure like that new movie with Harrison Ford. What was it?"

"*Indiana Jones and the Last Crusade*?"

"Yeah, that's it."

"Way better than that Back to the Future."

"You betcha. Time travelling. La-ame!"

"Anyway, like, I'm stoked to see where this leads."

"Totally, righteous, Liv. Hey, I'll check my app... I mean map." He drew a piece of paper from his back pocket.

App. Like, where'd that come from?

He studied the map. "This here was a major steal. It's a topographical map. Shows elevations and such. Totally rad."

"I knew I could count on you." She shoved his shoulder. "Whoa! It's the Zachinator. Workin' the map. Readin' the hills. Walkin' the trail. Dude, you're really rockin' it. Come on. Race you to that tree." Liv sped off, her Air Jordans flicking up bits of dirt and needles. Zach eyed her sweatpants, and what filled them, then sped after, quickly passing her and leading for some time until he skid to a stop.

"Whoa, dudette." He placed his hand up. He studied the map once more. "Look. There's where the path forks. Let's take this right one."

"Like, major OK with me. You're the navigator. Where's it go?

"It kinda peters out," he squinted, bringing the map closer, "but let's try it." He smiled at her. "Unless you're lame."

"Eat my shorts, butt-head."

"That's real grody. Heh, I've got some Whitesnake. Wanna listen? It ain't no house music."

"Righteous. Tune us up, Zach-Man."

Zach adjusted the volume on his Walkman as they started down the path. David Coverdale's rich voice echoed through the pines. It reminded Liv of the walk she and Zach were on, down some road they'd never been on. The trees dropped needles on the trail, softening the steps of Zach's black and white Hi Tops. The Walkman told them to make up their mind and stop wasting time.

As they strolled down the chosen trail a breeze swept needles and dirt into a small whirlwind around them. They coughed and flicked their hands. Liv wondered where that had suddenly come from. The squirrel squawked from its perch, trying to let them know.

The pines were planted in rows, a reforestation project from some time ago. Bark was peeling from the reddish trunks, which matched the off-coloured hue from the spiral design of Livy's tie-dye shirt. She had it tied in a knot in the front, showing her midriff. Her brown hair was cropped in a Pixie cut. She walked with her hands in the back pockets of her jeans.

The transistor radio made Fats Domino's voice sound tinny as he belted away his classic song, I'm Walking. Zachery gyrated to the music. "This guy is boss. It's a bummer we haven't seen him on stage." He removed his baseball cap and mopped his brow. His plaid blue shirt camouflaged with the lengthening shadows of the trees. He glanced to the west. "Still a few hours left. No need to split yet. This place is unreal."

"Neato! This place is so fab. If Te Rock was here, she'd freak out." Livy kicked at a small rock, her blue and red striped bell-bottom catching on her sandal. She flicked it off. "It's so quiet and relaxing, you just want to hang loose and enjoy. How much further?"

"Not too sure. I didn't bring a map, but we can keep going for a bit. It shouldn't get too hairy. Look, I see some birch trees up ahead."

Yes indeed, this is the Big Bassonie on C-H-A-M, Cham with a slam with the best of today's music on 820 AM.

That was Fats Domino with Walkin' and now here we go with some more movement and Ray Charles having to Hit The Road, Jack.

"That Ray is so groovy. Whenever he plays, he looks so jazzed."

"Fab. Saw him on Ed Sullivan. Jamming with some guitarist. Can't remember his name. It was outta sight, though. Say, did you see Kennedy bragging about going to the moon?"

"Yeah. He's just a kiss up. Probably gone when he said that. Nobody will ever walk on the moon. Take too much scratch. His old lady is outta sight, though."

"Ooh, the Zach-meister. Eying the first lady. Trying to make me jealous?"

"Naa, just saying." His face flushed. He flicked his head, the Brylcreem infused curl centering nicely on his forehead. "Hey, this radio's a downer. Poor reception." He adjusted the knob.

"Changing the subject, are we. You're such a flake."

"What'd you say?"

"I said you're such a flake. Just jokin'. Don't get heavy on me."

"OK, solid. Let's get going. We don't want to get stuck on this trail."

Livy moved toward Zachery and he held out his hand. They skipped down the trail watching the trees and birds. The squirrel darted out on the path scolding them for intruding on his domain. It sat for a second and scampered up a tree where it continued its onslaught of accusations. The radio got more staticky and Zachery turned it off. The path narrowed as they entered a section of Birch trees.

Olivia twisted her parasol to look at the squirrel. "Such a chatty animal, Zachariah, don't you think? What is he saying, my love?"

"I don't know for sure, but he should be saying you have eyes so beautiful and lips so red and flowing hair only a goddess could own. It should be saying you are the single most beautiful creature in all creation."

"Oh Zachariah, you're teasing me. Don't stop, though." She looked at his powder blue jacket, ruffled white shirt and dark blue bow tie. His grey fedora covered a closely cropped head of chestnut brown hair. "This is such a lovely afternoon, isn't it?

He smiled at her. Olivia sported a rose patterned A-line dress with puffed shoulders. Her blonde curls flowed out from beneath her red and white skimmer hat. "Yes, my dear, especially when I'm with you." He offered his arm, and she slid her hand through grasping his forearm. The squirrel gave one final warning, then scurried away.

Tall Birch trees surrounded them as they strolled down the trail. Smaller bushes closed in on the path creating a wall of vegetation. Olivia snuggled closer, laying her head on Zachariah's shoulder. They walked for several minutes, enjoying the quiet and serenity. "It's so beautiful here." She raised her head and looked at him. "Promise me it will always be like this. Always. You will promise, won't you?"

"Of course, my love." He looked into her eyes. "I promise to protect you. I promise to always love you. Just like this trail, our lives will be perfect."

"Oh Zachariah, you are so wonderful." She squeezed his arm and listened to the rustling of the bushes. They seemed to be singing to her. She was sure she heard something about some trails being happy and some were blue. It was odd.

The skies were turning a darker shade as the sun caressed the western horizon. Olivia turned to her loved one. "Zachariah, my dear. Shall we head back? It's getting late."

"Of course, lovey-dovey. We must make it back before dark. It's not far though. We should make good time." They turned to head back as a zephyr of breeze shook the trees again. They sang out to them. Olivia heard that song again. About happy trails. Then it whispered that this one would be the end.

The bushes had grown over the path they had come from. Small branches twisted and twirled over the trail. New roots took hold and formed more brushes as the path was overgrown. The wall of foliage crept towards them. Zachariah spun around. The same was happening behind them.

Olivia brought a white-gloved hand to her mouth stifling a scream. "Zachariah, what's happening? Do something."

"Olivia, my love, I don't know. It's some bedevilment, no doubt. Stay close."

Brushes closed in on them, intertwining along the path, whispering to them. Olivia's gloved hand could not muffle the screaming as the smaller branches encircled their bodies. The sun waved a final goodbye as it snuck below the horizon. The screaming stopped and the only sound was a soft lullaby as the bushes settled in for the night.

They sang of happy trails.

FROM ALL SIDES

This story is written in reverse chronological order, similar to Shimmer Lake or Donny Darko.

Friday, June 26, 11:37 PM

Sergeant Detective Jenny Downey typed the last few words of her report and hit PRINT. She arched her back, arms stretched out at her sides, and stifled a yawn. The Malone report finished printing and she signed the last page and dropped it into the Captain's 'IN' basket.

"All done?" asked her partner, Gary Johnson.

"Not quite. Still need to go over my notes from today. Where's Fred?"

"Downstairs, logging evidence. He'll be another half hour or so." Gary grabbed his jacket and swung it over his shoulder with one finger. "Well, I'm outta here. See you Monday."

"Yeah, Gary. Remember, Chico's at nine for breakfast."

"Will do."

Jenny pulled out her notebook and tried transcribing them but couldn't concentrate. Losing her latest case still nagged at her. A major crime figure got off on a technicality. She slammed her notebook closed, thought about bringing it home, then locked it in her desk. Not what she needed this weekend. She grabbed her purse and headed out of the office.

Jenny pushed on the release bar of the side door of the 5th Division and stepped into the fresh night air, a relief from the oppressive heat of the day. Two small maples, freshly planted this spring, bracketed the short sidewalk to the parking lot. At least two dozen cars remained in the well-lit lot, a reminder that the cop shop never slept.

It had been a long day-- four open cases, the captain demanding results, and no end in sight. She was looking forward to getting home and relaxing with a long, hot bath, and some red wine. Since her divorce, several months ago, downtime was important to her. She clicked her fob and noticed a flash of light to her right. It looked far off, just a tiny glint. She stared a bit, then backed up a step. There, again. It was like a reflection, similar to the sun off a mirror. It was coming from a car centered between two others near the other end of the lot.

Binoculars? She craned her neck from side to side and another flash appeared. The car was occupied, she could see that much, but the headlight and interior lights were off. She was on full alert now, trying to get a read on the situation. The car started up and crept out of the parking lot. Once out on the street, it sped up and disappeared around the corner. She grabbed her phone and dialed.

"Hey Fred. Probably nothing but there was a later model Rav parked at the far end of the lot. Blue, or black. Someone sitting in it. If I had to guess, scoping us out. When they noticed I was giving them the stink-eye, they took off." ... "Yeah, could be Louie, who knows." ... "Don't worry, I'll keep an eye out." ... "You too. See you Monday."

She pocketed her cell and with a final look around, slid into the driver's seat. The engine fired up and she cranked on some tunes. She eased out of the lot and into traffic, a quick look for anyone following her. With nothing in sight, she settled into the seat and listened to the radio.

Fifteen minutes later she pulled into her driveway and hit the remote for the garage. She parked inside, closed the door, and got out of the car. It was a two-bay, with plenty of room for someone to hide, and she had another look around.

You're getting paranoid, Downey. She chuckled to herself and opened the side door to her three bedroom back-split, flicked on the lights and canceled the alarm. Having second thoughts, she reset it. She eyed the fridge, decided against the wine for now, and headed upstairs. She took a quick shower to remove the grime, her firearm and badge locked in her safe. She filled the tub adding some bubbles for a relaxing soak.

Ten minutes later she was soaking in the tub, thinking about the last year. Overshadowing it all, was the bitter divorce. Finalized in November, it had been a horrible six-month battle. Her marriage had been good for the first five years but slid downhill the next three. Mark had been abusive, emotionally rather than physically, and jealous of her success as a police officer, while he was stuck in a mediocre, dead-end job. They had argued about children, money, vacations, and anything else that was convenient. Finally, enough was enough and she had demanded a divorce.

Then there was her promotion to Sergeant and the recent partially unresolved human trafficking case, and the list went on and on.

She cleared this from her mind and concentrated on happy thoughts as she slid underwater, holding her breath. Several seconds passed before she came up for air. Her eyes opened when she felt a plastic bag pulled over her head. It sealed around her mouth as she tried to draw in a breath. She tried ripping the bag with her hands. Her wrists were clasped and she was dragged out of the tub. Her head struck the tile floor, then her hips. She started to blackout and her assailant straddled her, wrapped his hands around her throat, and started to squeeze. She shook her head trying to stay conscious and managed to form a small air pocket in the bag, drawing in recycled air. The attacker bashed her head repeatedly against the tile as their hands tightened around her neck. It would not be long before she blacked out. Instincts took over and she reached out and clawed at his bare arms, hoping for some DNA evidence under her nails. Maybe they can still catch him even if I'm dead. She had no doubt it was a man. He was powerful and bulky. She was able to draw her nails down his left forearm, peeling off skin as she saw the blurry image of a Mickey Mouse tattoo.

Soon after that she passed out, then died, her head bashed in, blood pooling in the bag and leaking onto the floor.

***

Friday, June 26, 7:45 PM

Earlier that evening, the man known as "Gryphon" dried the last of his dishes and placed them in the cupboards of his elaborately laid out kitchen. His house covered close to six thousand square feet on a twenty-acre lot surrounded by Crown Land. He often thought about hiring a maid or cook but did not want the hassle of keeping his business hidden. Gryphon was a private man and liked the solitary life. His nearest neighbor was seven kilometers away, a convenient situation when he decided to use his outdoor range. He practiced often. Gryphon was a contract killer, and a good one.

The kitchen lights shut off automatically as he walked down the hall. A procession of automatic lights flicked on and off lighting his way to his office. He smiled as he thought about his house, the little eccentric additions he requested from the contractors, motion lights, voice-activated gadgets, superior alarm system, heated indoor pool with sauna and hot tub, as well as his indoor and outdoor shooting ranges. The latter two were installed by some discreet contractors known to him from previous clients. All in all, a good setup for this side of his life. Gryphon led a double life, this one of a contract killer, and his other, where he maintained the status quo, a regular job, and an apartment.

He sat in front of his computer and read over the details on his current contract. He couldn't believe it. Actually, two contracts. Two different people wanting the same person dead. Double payment for the same job. And it was going to be an easy one. He had enough information now and decided it was time. Tonight, if everything went well, or tomorrow. He sent the information through a complex series of servers onto the "dark web" then scrubbed the hard drive. He walked over to a bookcase and reached behind and pressed a button. The bookcase swung outward, revealing a steel door with a punch pad. He entered the code and the door opened to a room ten by twenty feet, lined with shelves containing handguns, sniper rifles, surveillance equipment, and several cases. He chose a large carrying case containing all the necessary items for tonight. It was his "Close Quarters" case, containing a garrote, knives, handguns, and clean up materials. He closed the door, replaced the bookcase, and walked to the seven-car garage.

Gryphon had a few wrecks he used during jobs. Tonight, he chose a 2014 dark blue Toyota Rav4. It was registered to a person who had died four years ago. Gryphon never went out on a job with a vehicle registered in either of his names. He drove down out his gate and activated the perimeter security.

He accelerated down the road into the city, where he navigated into a suburban area and parked under a broken streetlight along Glanville Ave. He had broken it two days ago. There were no cars in the driveway, no lights on except the front porch. He smiled. Why did people put on their porch light when they left their house? It was a dead giveaway that they were not home. You could never be too sure, so he waited a while longer, observing the neighborhood. The street was dead. Not many cars drove by after dark.

He checked his watch. The after-work dog walkers were settled back in their homes, the last-pee dog walkers wouldn't be out until 10:30-11:00. Time to check if the owner was home. He exited the car and walked down the sidewalk, crossing the street, and approached without hesitation. He knew the layout well. Double car driveway and garage, four steps up to a small porch at the front entrance. Another door inside the garage and one at the back. Living room, dining room, kitchen and two-piece bath on the main floor. Three bedrooms and a full bath on the upper split in the back. He had entered from around the back through a glass sliding door with an easy lock. The alarm had not been that hard. He had a scanner that deciphered the code and disabled it. The readout allowed him to reset it upon leaving. He peered in, trying to determine if she were home or not. Satisfied she was not, he strolled back to the car and got in. He checked his watch and started the car, accelerating from the curb.

Twenty minutes later he pulled into the parking lot of the 5th Division and parked between two cars at the far end. A couple of dozen cars remained there, including hers. He shut his engine off and checked his watch. It was 10:57 and he sat waiting for some indication she would be heading home. At 11:41 a figure strolled out of the side door, a suit jacket thrown over his shoulder. Gryphon watched through binoculars as Detective Gary Johnson got in his car and drove away. Fifteen minutes later the side door opened again, and a woman walked out, hands in the back pockets of her jeans. She pulled out her keys. The lights on her car blinked twice and the interior light came on. Then she looked in his direction and stopped. She continued to stare as he tossed the binoculars in the passenger seat and started the car. He drove out of the parking lot, then sped up when he was out on the street, heading back towards Glanville Ave.

***

Monday, June 22, 6:09 PM

Mark Downey sat on his lumpy couch stewing over the last year of his life. A "rent overdue" notice had arrived in the mail. It was her fault. That Bitch. Divorcing him like that. Right out of the blue. He'd been served the papers at work, too: that was the real kicker. Sure, they'd had some arguments, but what couple didn't? He wanted kids, she didn't. She was a miser with the money, and he liked to live a little. Nothing wrong with that, right? She was always jamming it down his throat how much more she made. Couldn't he find a better paying job. Well, he had been trying, but jobs were scarce. She just had the Golden Touch, and he had to work his tail off for everything. Hadn't it been him that had stayed home and kept the place running while she ran around at all hours trying to get promoted. He was the one that had always made the home better. Sure, she cleaned and cooked on the weekends, but that was just because she felt guilty. He knew she would rather be running around with her boyfriend detectives.

Mark stood and walked into the kitchen. He pulled out a frozen dinner and stuck it in the microwave. He had an hour or two before he had to leave for work. Damn job. A janitor at Home Depot. Sweep the floors, clean the toilets, mop here, dust there. He had asked for a different job, anything with more money. He wanted to be on the floor, customer assistant, restocking, anything, but no. They wouldn't budge an inch. 'Oh no, Mr. Downey. Of course not.' Just one little cussing out of a customer and it follows you for life. 'No contact with the customers.' Bastards. Now I have to work the night shift. He supposed it could be worse. At least he still had a job. Yeah, but a stinkin' job, a stinkin' apartment, a stinkin' life. All because of her.

The microwave ding brought him out of his thoughts and he pulled out the hot meal, burning his fingers in the process. He got it onto the counter and cursed some more, sucking his fingers. He worked the microwave dish onto a regular plate and headed back into the living room. *Who was he kidding? This was no living room.* It was an extension of the kitchen. In fact, the dump was just three rooms, the kitchen/living room combo, the bedroom, and the bathroom, for a total of 450 square feet.

He turned on the TV by hand, he had lost the remote during the move, and adjusted the antenna. Cable was too expensive, so he relied on rabbit ears to get the three channels he watched. The news was on and he half watched, fuming at everything. He ate some of his dinner and gagged, spitting it up back into the tray. He shuddered, then leaned back on the couch, put his hands behind his head and closed his eyes. Several deep breaths settled him down and he leaned forward staring at the package on the coffee table.

The package included a phone he'd bought for cash at some fleabag discount store. He picked up the little cardboard box and opened it. Inside, the plastic wrapping was a different story. The packaging was a literal Fort Knox. He fumbled with it for a minute before he screamed and threw the package across the room. It slid under the fridge. He pounded his temples with his wrists, rocking back and forth on the couch, and then bolted into the kitchen. He threw open a drawer, choosing a large butcher knife.

You want to mess with me? I'll slice you open, you bastard. For one brief moment he considered to what, or whom, he was directing his anger, then he fished out the phone and hacked at the plastic packaging until he could pry it open and retrieve the contents. He fumbled with the SIM card and phone, dropping each several times. He managed not to throw anything and walked back to the couch, slowing his breathing. After a couple of minutes, he focused on the task and managed to insert the card and battery. When he pushed the power button, nothing happened. He checked to see if the battery was installed properly and tried again. Still nothing. Slamming the phone down, he stood up and kicked the couch. "God damned useless secondhand crap store." Stomping over to the kitchen, he banged his forehead against the fridge, screaming. Someone above him stomped on their floor. He was about to yell at them when he saw the phone charger laying in the packaging. He whacked his palm to his forehead. *Stupid. Stupid. Stupid.* He blew through his clenched teeth, then wrestled the charger out. The phone had ended up on the tattered rug and he grabbed it and plugged in the charger. He used the five minutes it took before the phone beeped to calm down and fish out the number Benny had given him. His fingers shook as he dialed.

Monday, June 22, 1:37 PM

David Ford checked his watch and began to clear his desk in preparation for his after-lunch customer. He worked as a travel agent in a small strip mall on Chestnut street. He preferred this to one of the more prominent locations someone in his profession might desire. David made very good coin and could afford to set his own hours. He had the occasional walk-in but most of his customers were appointments through referrals. Right on time the gentleman entered the store and approached the desk.

"Mr. Ford?"

"Yes. Have a seat. How can I help you today?"

"Well, as I said on the phone, I wish to book a trip to one of those working farm vacations in Argentina. For myself, my wife, and our two boys. For a month, over the Christmas break."

"I've got a couple of choices up on the screen, for you to have a look at. As you can see..."

An hour later everything was booked, and another satisfied customer walked out the door. David checked his watch. Almost four. Time to close it down and head to the gym. He shut down his computer, locked his desk, lowered the blinds, and flipped over the closed sign, before locking the door and walking to his car. Arms and legs today, with a little cardio.

***

David sat in his lazy-boy sipping a brandy watching the 6:30 news. The anchor was a bimbo, but he considered this station the most reliable, so he put up with her blonde coif, annoying nasal squeak, and irritating habit of tapping her fingers to emphasize a point. *"The Dow Jones fell 47 points today..." Tap, tap, tap. "... and analysts predict a rebound by this Friday." Tap, tap, tap.* A basketball game was on later and he figured his team had a good chance.

One of his cell phones-- he had three of them, rang. It was the red one, the one that rang for special occasions. He placed his brandy down, checked his watch, and picked the phone up, looking at the number. As he thought, it said 'private number'. He answered anyway.

"Hello?"

"Is th... this G... G... Gryphon?"

"It could be. I need a name from you."

"F... f..."

"Not your real name, idiot."

"Oh yeah. K... Kelvin S...smith."

"Ok, Kelvin Smith, what would you like?"

"I need someone k... killed."

"Do you, now. That's quite interesting. What's that got to do with me?" He checked his watch again.

"I heard y... you do that s...sort of thing."

"If I did that sort of thing, and I'm not saying I do, I would probably want all the money upfront, hypothetically, that is. So, if *You* were to kill anyone for someone else, how much would *You* want, hypothetically?

"M... maybe t... twenty thousand?"

"Well, I would consider you an amateur and not capable of doing the job properly. As a matter of fact, I would think you were only able to get one-fifth of the job done, like hurt an arm, or a leg, but not hypothetically kill anyone. Not that I'm suggesting I would know anything about how much a person would want to kill another. Just shooting the breeze."

"Ok. I c... can come up with a h... hundred g... grand."

"So, hypothetically, if someone were to do this, I've seen on TV that they sometimes leave phones taped to the underside of tables somewhere. I must admit, I watch way too much TV, though. Anyways, do you know Cliffy's Chowdown? They make a mean BLT. Every day at 2:15 Cliffy puts on a taped soccer game, usually Tottenham. The best place to watch it from is the back booth. Anyways about what you called about, sorry I can't help you Kelvin."

"Okay, G...Gryphon."

"Bye now." David hung up and checked his watch. 7:12. Time to pour another drink before tip-off.

***

Thursday, June 18, 2:14 PM

"Foreman of the jury, have you reached a decision?"

"Yes we have, your honor."

"What say you?"

"On the charges of seven counts of human trafficking, we find the defendant, Louis Lefebvre, *not guilty*." There was mumbling around the court room. Jenny Downy threw up her hands and looked at her partner Gary.

"What the hell!" she whispered. The judge's gavel rapped three times.

"Quiet down! Please continue."

"On the charges of kidnapping, we find the defendant, *not guilty*."

"On the charges of forcible confinement, we find the defendant, *not guilty*."

Judge Hargrave addressed the jurors over the buzz in the crowd. "You are now dismissed. This court thanks you for your service." He rapped his gavel again. "Court is adjourned. Mr. Lefebvre, you are free to go."

Jenny jumped out of her seat in the packed courtroom. "That's impossible. That bastard! How'd he do it?" Her colleagues eyed her.

"Relax, Jenny. It was probably the partial. Don't worry. He'll screw up. We'll get him." It was Gary Johnson. He grabbed an elbow to guide her out. "Let's go." She shook him off.

"Let go of me." She walked to the edge of the rail dividing the spectators from the defendant. Louis Lefebvre glanced at her with a smile. He pointed, then brought his thumb up to his throat, drawing it slowly across his neck. He raised an eyebrow and nodded twice, then walked through the gate, maintaining eye contact as long as possible before walking out of the court a free man.

Jenny wanted to go after him, but she was grabbed by her coworkers. "Let it go," Gary said. "Come on. I'll take you for a beer."

"I don't want a beer." Jenny snapped back. "I wanna nail that sucker."

"You can start tomorrow." It was Dan Ridley, Captain of the squad. "Go. Go have a drink and let off some steam. That's an order. Clear your mind."

Gary steered her to the exit. "I think we'll forget about the beer and go straight to tequila.

"Yeah, whatever."

Jenny felt her partners eyes on her until she settled down on the walk to the parking lot. He'd been her partner for two years now, and he'd seen the decline in her marriage, the divorce, and now the frustration with this case. He was good people. "Come on," he said. "We'll have a few at Casey's and call it a night."

"Okay Gare. I'm good now. We'll go have a few." She walked around to the passenger's side. "You drive."

They seated themselves near the back in a booth and ordered beers and shots. Not much light filtered through the stained, glass windows making the place dreary. A couple of other detectives were at the bar and two uniformed cops ate at another booth.

"Want any donuts, too?" asked the waiter.

"Real funny, Jimmy. Those are for the Uni's." Jenny flicked her hand, dismissing him. She looked at Gary. "That expert witness screwed us over."

"Yeah, but I have to give it to that defense lawyer. He tore the witnesses apart. Broke them down badly. That and the partial fingerprint did leave some reasonable doubt."

"Not in my mind."

"Not in mine, either, but we don't get a vote."

Jenny sighed. "Think he got to some of them?"

"The jurors. Yeah, probably. He's got pull, that's for sure. Anyways, let's talk about something else.

"Like what?"

"Like… how's the new home coming along?"

"You've asked me that a million times. Everything is set up, organized, and it even *feels* like home now. I've started to work on a garden. It's as 'coming' as it's going to get."

He turned his head and smiled. "You? A garden."

"Yeah me." She gave him a shove. "Why not me?"

"Sgt. Jennifer Downey, green thumb, extraordinaire."

"Go to hell." She leaned back and took a slow sip of her beer. "Did you see what that scumbag did when he was leaving?"

"The slit-your-throat thing. Yeah, I saw it. He wouldn't dare." Gary scrunched his face for a moment.

"At least not him." Jenny commented. "He couldn't do the dirty work, but he might hire someone who could."

"Just watch your back. Want a detail put on you?"

"No, I'll be fine. I'd love him to come after me."

"Yeah," Gary smiled. "You'll hit him with a tomato from your garden. Wipe him right out."

"Ah, shut up." She grabbed her tequila. "You drinking, or flapping your gums. Let's go." She downed the shot and waved at Jimmy to bring some more.

***

Louis 'Two Toes' Lefebvre sat on an expensive leather couch in an upstairs office of one of his clubs. He had changed out of his suit into comfortable jeans, a pull-over sweater, and a buttoned-up shirt. On his feet were alligator skin boots that came to a point. Nose Pickers, he called them. The name 'Two Toes' came from an unfortunate encounter with a chisel wielded by the torturer of one of his competitors when he was just breaking into the trade. It had been hard relearning how to walk with only his two small toes on each foot. It was harder still on his competition when revenge was extracted three years later. It involved a drill and wood bit. Now he had 'Pinky' LaChance, the 6" 4', 300-pound body guard to his right. Seated in a couch to the left was Louis's new lieutenant, Bobby Simpson.

"So, you say he's good?" Louis said to Bobby.

"Word on the street is he's the best, Louis."

"Good. I want that meddling bitch gone. Today was a close one. We'll need to be careful, for a while. How many in the queue?"

"We have seven coming from Montreal, three from Vancouver, and the new contact from Detroit is proving his worth. Seventeen."

Louis's grinned maliciously. "Do we have the room?"

"Should have. If not, we'll just double them up. They're just whores."

"Well, let's be extra careful."

There was a knock on the door.

"What is it?" Louis barked.

A thin man entered. "He's here, sir."

"Send him in." Louis watched a man enter and stand in front of him. Grey eyes that bored right through you. Dressed casually but not shabbily. On closer look he saw the muscles underneath. Not body-builder size, more sinewy, a man that could take care of himself. The man waited in front of them, not quite slouched, but with a casualness Louis despised.

"What's your name?" Louis asked.

"I don't have a name, but you can call me Sam." He checked his watch. "What would you like from me?"

"I need a certain person eliminated. Are you capable of such an endeavor?"

Sam looked at the other two, then back at Louis. "No. I think you are mistaken."

Louis looked at the man, checking for any signs of weakness, any wavering. All he got was an unnerving vibe, a coldness. He nodded to his men and they left the room. "Have a seat. Would you like a drink?"

Sam sat down, eyes shifting around. "I'll have a brandy."

Louis went to the bar and poured two drinks, handing one to Sam. "So, can you help me, or do I need to go somewhere else?"

"I may have some availability over a limited window but there's a high surcharge for a quick turnaround. And," his eyes fixed on Louis's, "the money's up front. All of it. Who's the mark?" He took a sip of the brandy and nodded his approval.

"A detective at the 5th Division."

"I see." Sam reached into his pocket and drew out a blank card and pen. He wrote down a number and handed it to Louis.

'Two Toes' read the number and smiled. "Will cash do?"

"Preferably."

"Good. The person..." Louis was interrupted by Sam raising his hand, then pointing to the card. He smiled and wrote on the card. "Here you go, 'Sam'. I hope that is enough information?" Sam nodded. "Good, now the question of your wages. Just one second." 'Two Toes' looked up to the corner of the room and waved his fingers.

On cue, Bobby came through the door with two briefcases. He placed them on the bar and transferred the correct amount from one to the other and walked over to the two men. Sam was checking his watch. Bobby set the briefcase on the table. Sam opened it and rifled through the contents, nodded, closed the briefcase and stood.

He glanced at Louis. “I’ll call you.”

“Looking forward to it.” He smiled and watched ‘Sam’ walk out the door. Moments later ‘Pinky’ came back in.

“We all good?” said Bobby.

“Very much so, gentlemen.” Louise leaned back on the couch and clapped his hands, rubbing them. “Let’s celebrate, shall we?” Pinky went to pour some drinks and distributed them. Louis raised his glass. “To whores, money, and a corrupt justice system.” They raised their glasses and repeated his toast. “May they flourish forever.”

***

Friday, January 17th, 11:00AM

Six months earlier, Jenny, her partner, and several others from the squad were gathered in the conference room. Against precinct rules, Gary had smuggled in some beer for the occasion, although nothing had been consumed yet. Everyone was still backslapping and shaking hands. Captain Dan Ridley walked to the head of the table, a smile on his face, and raised his hands.

“All right everyone. Let’s settle down. I’ve got a couple of announcements to make.”

“Ya think so,” someone yelled out. Laughter sprung out again.

“Okay, okay. I guess we should get the trivial stuff out of the way first. As you all know, we were able to infiltrate a prostitute trafficking ring and arrest two of the top leaders.” A cheer rose from the group. “‘Lefty’ Malone and Louis ‘Two Toes’ Lefebvre were apprehended a few weeks ago and have been arraigned. I just got word from the DA. ‘Lefty’s trial is set for March 27th and Louis’s for Jun 8th.” Another roar. Dan raised his hands again and it slowly quieted down. “There’s still lots of work to do. We need to go over the evidence and tighten the noose around these bastards before it goes to trial, but for now, time for a little celebration.”

“Hey, Cappy. You said this was the trivial news. What could be more important than this?”

“Ah, yes. Almost forgot.”

"Yeah, you're always forgetting." A roar broke out from the group. Dan raised his hands again.

"As you know, Ed retired last December, and we've been without a squad sergeant since then." The room became silent. "After careful consideration, and in consultation with the chief, I have appointed the new squad sergeant." There were glances around, some with hopeful grins and raised eyebrows. "For their tireless efforts all the time, but especially during this investigation, the new sergeant for the squad is... detective... Jenny Downey!" A unanimous cheer went up. Jenny was grabbed by four of her colleagues and raised above their heads. They bounced her and slowly brought her to the front and set her down by the captain. He shook her hand and pinned the sergeant's collar dogs on her. "May I present Detective Sergeant Jenny Downey."

For the next half hour handshakes were exchanged, congratulations given out and war stories told. Everyone settled in chairs around the table and the beers began to flow. As much as she tried to hold them back, a few tears rolled down her cheeks. She made her way around the table, stopping to exchange stories with her co-workers, accepting congratulations and wondering what the new responsibilities would bring. She had hoped to be the one named, but never thought she would get it. Now there would be additional pressure on her to perform, but she welcomed it.

***

He sat sipping on a beer, watching the fiasco. All this commotion over *Her*. He deserved the promotion more than she did. More time in, longer in the squad. It was a token promotion, one to meet the establishment's quota. Probably screwing the captain. And the chief. God, he hated her.

Look at her, strutting her stuff, shaking her ass… It was disgusting. He downed his beer, crushed the can, and grabbed another. Twenty-four years in and he had been passed over again. He stared across the table at nothing in particular, thinking back on his career. Nothing stood out, nothing he had done wrong. It should have been him.

There was only one reason why he'd been passed up, and it infuriated him. He sat there, his anger festering, as a plan began to formulate. The details filled in, as if by themselves and he had it figured out in ten minutes -- except one crucial thing.

Then he remembered the evidence room. Lots of money stored away there. He chugged his beer, spilling some on his forearm and slammed the beer down. A couple of people gave him a cursory glance before returning to their banter. He wiped the beer from his tattooed arm and got up to 'congratulate' his new sergeant. She had six months to enjoy her new job.

Saturday, December 7, 1:30 PM

A month before her promotion, Detective Jenny Downey pulled up to the curb by the two-story Tudor on Denver Avenue. Dozens of cars lined the street and she saw Gary Johnson, her work partner, getting out of one of them. They were meeting at their captain's house to celebrate the retirement of Ed Torrey, squad sergeant. She grabbed her macaroni casserole and met Gary at the driveway entrance.

"What ja bring?"

"Chocolate cake. You?"

"The usual."

"Ed's car's here. He's probably half in the bag by now."

"Yeah, this one's a freebie. No spouses so he can let his hair down."

"Jenny, I think you forgot. Ed doesn't have any hair." They both chuckled as they made their way along the side of the house, into the back yard. The smell of barbequed steaks drifted over to them. Roughly two dozen men and women were on the patio and spread out onto the grass, mingling in little clusters.

"Hey, it's the dynamic duo!" some yelled.

Dan Ridley, their squad captain, called out. "Hey, you two. Welcome. Food goes in the kitchen. Through that sliding door. Beer's in the cooler over there. Hard stuff is inside."

Jenny negotiated the glass door, balancing the salad, and placed it in the fridge. She came back out and grabbed a beer and wandered over to Dan.

"Where's Fred? I don't see him."

"I sent him on beer run. Eddy's using a funnel today. I'm glad he has a ride home. How do you like your steak?"

"Medium's fine. Good turnout."

"Yeah, Ed made a lot of friends." Dan paused and looked at her. "Hey, Benny's here..."

"What?"

"Don't start anything. Ed asked him. Benny was his CI." Jenny pursed her lips. When did confidential informants get invited to police socials? "I didn't know he was coming, or I would have said something. Ed figured he couldn't come to the official retirement party, so he asked him to come today."

"Jesus Christ, Dan." She flung her hands up, spilling beer. "He knows about Benny and my ex. What the hell?"

"Hey, listen. This is not about you. It's Ed's retirement party. Play it cool. Put your big-girl panties on and suck it up."

Jenny scowled, but backed off. He was about the only person here that could get away with a comment like that without getting popped. She respected him, and therefore held back.

She thought back to the time that Benny and her ex, Mark, had been caught pilfering phones from a warehouse. At the time he was still her husband and things had not yet turned for the worse. Dan had let things slide for Mark because of Jenny, and Ed had struck a deal to use Benny as a CI. Mark had promised her he would stay away from Benny, but she knew different. Just another of the many reasons for her and Mark splitting. Divorce was still a touchy subject for her, it being only a month ago. She forced a smile on her face.

"No problem. I'll behave."

"Good. Now go mingle before I burn a steak, here."

Jenny wandered in amongst the others, catching up on the latest. She made her way over to Ed, who was surrounded by several detectives telling a bunch of war stories. She reached out and shook hands.

"Say, old timer. How are ya doing?"

"Fine. Fine. How's the trafficking case going?"

"It's going well. We got the two main jerks in custody and still collecting evidence, but I think we're solid."

"Great! And how is the...?" He hesitated. "the divorce coming?"

She glanced in the direction of Benny, who was occupied with some others several feet away. "It's done. Found a house. Take possession the first of February. Things are getting better."

"That's good to hear Jenny." He placed a hand on her shoulder. "That'll be a bugger, moving in the winter."

"Well, yeah," She looked around the back yard. "But I'll have lots of help. If we can have a barbeque in the winter, we can move in the winter." She glanced at his arm. Say what the hell is that?"

"It's a new tat. My grandkids love it. Say ..."

The group yelled out and cheered, then a chant began. "FINE A LEE, FINE A LEE." Jenny spun around and saw Fred Winkley and two others carrying several cases of beer into the yard. She smiled then looked back at Ed. "Say what are you going to do now? Loaf around and get fat?"

He stared at her for a second. "Actually, I've been hired by the government. It's rather secret work and if I told you, I'd have to kill you." He stared at her for another ten seconds before he burst out laughing. "Ha. I'm getting into the security business. You know, house alarms and such. Always like messing around with those electronics."

Jenny managed a smile, unsure how to respond.

"Hey, I could do your new house if you wanted?"

"Sure thing, Ed." She relaxed "We'll talk." She felt someone come up beside her. Fred Winkley reached around her to grasp Ed's hand and shook it.

"H... how's it g... going old m... man?"

"Great." Ed answered. "And you?"

"G... good." Fred looked at Jenny. "And y... you?"

"I'm doing fine, Fred." She thought of something else to say. Fred's stutter always made her uncomfortable. "Thanks for the beer run." She looked around. "Looks like they're all going to be drunk."

"F... for a good c... cause, I'd s... say." He lightly punched Ed on the shoulder. "C... con... g... grad... ulations."

"Ah, it was nothing, working with people like you and Jenny." He waved his arm around, sloshing some beer. "Hell, all these people."

"W... what's that?" He pointed to Ed's arm.

Jenny piped up. "That's his new tattoo. He says it's for his grand kids."

"M... maybe. Same p... place as m... mine. At least m... mine's more m… manly." Fred laughed.

Ed joined in. “Well, that’s true. But I think the stupidest one, pardon me Jenny, was your ex’s. Why in hell would anyone get a Mickey Mouse tattooed on his arm? You didn’t even have kids, did you?”

Jenny was lost in thought. I never did like that tattoo.

THE INVESTIGATION

This story follows From All Sides and is in normal Chronological order.

It was close to one AM. when Gryphon rolled down Glanville Avenue and stopped under the broken streetlamp. This section of the avenue was in darkness. Most lights were off in the houses and the street was dead. In the backsplit, there was one faded light on – it looked like the main bathroom upstairs. Gryphon checked his watch. In all his years as a hitman, he had never had a mark quite like this.

He surveyed the area one last time. Everything quiet. The only difference he noted was a car parked about two hundred feet down the street. He'd never seen it before, but it was the weekend and maybe someone had visitors. This disturbed him somewhat, he decided to continue with the job and walked over to the house, carrying his case.

Around the back, he picked the lock, opened the glass sliding door, and went to disarm the alarm. Strange. It hadn't been activated. This mark was getting sloppy. He laid his case on the dining table and retrieved the garrote. This would leave an impression. He grabbed the well-worn handles and snapped the wire taught a couple of times. It felt good.

He was about to screw on his silencer when he heard a shuffling noise and spun around. A figure stood at the far kitchen entrance. It grabbed something from the counter and charged him. Gryphon fumbled with the silencer just as a ceramic flowerpot smashed on his head. It shattered, dirt flying everywhere.

Gryphon fired his gun, blinking his eyes clear. The glass sliding door crashed as the bullet flew through it. His jaw was sliced as momentum carried them to the ground. A chair tumbled over. *What a shit show.* He kicked his legs, trying to remove the man. The assailant's hands wrapped around his throat. He managed to work his gun free and fired three shots into the side of the body. *Die, you fucker.* The man screamed and went limp. Gryphon wiggled sideways and shoved the man off.

Shit. Shit, shit, shit. He felt his jaw and looked at his hand. Lots of blood. The guy was bleeding out on the rug. Gryphon calmed himself and listened. There was no noise from upstairs. *Where was the mark? Who was this guy?* He'd checked this place out thoroughly. She lived alone and never had visitors.

He looked at his gun. Hadn't had time to screw on the silencer. *Man, what a mess. Okay, just a quick look to see where the mark is.*

A siren in the distance changed those plans.

He packed up the kit and ran out the door with his case. Lights were on in several of the houses. He rushed to his car and sped off, using a roundabout route to get to his countryside retreat.

With the car safely stored in the garage, he went into his house and addressed his cut. It needed medical attention, beyond his skills. He knew of a very discrete doctor that owed him some favors. He grabbed for his phone but could not find it. Had he lost it in the scuffle? It was his red phone and that spelled trouble. He used another and called his colleague.

Three hours later he was stitched up but in a foul mood. The doctor had left. He sat with a brandy mulling over the night. He could not sleep.

***

It wasn't until four a.m. that Detective Gary Johnson was informed of the murder of his partner. Jenny had been found dead on her bathroom floor. He raced over to the scene where a multitude of cars were parked, including police cruisers and the coroner's. Yellow tape surrounded the house on Glanville. He flashed his badge and ducked under the tape. Dan Ridley, the squad captain intercepted him with hands raised.

"No, no, no. You're too close to this. Fred's taking lead. You go back home."

Gary drew Dan aside and whispered. "Christ, Cappy. Fred can't even speak, and that greenhorn he has for a partner needs his diaper changed every half hour. Let me go in and have a look." There was a hitch in Gary's voice. "Please."

Dan scrunched his right cheek and turned his head to the side. "Alright, go have a quick look." Gary went to leave but Dan grabbed his arm. "Fred's lead on this. Don't be stirring up any shit."

Gary raised his hands. "Just double-checking everything."

"Well, double-check without ruffling any feathers." Dan grabbed his arm again. "Hey, sorry about this. I know you were close."

"Ya," Gary scowled. "But not close enough. We should have put a detail on her. Most likely Louis?"

"I'm not so sure. Her ex is in there. Dead."

"Shit." Gary scrambled away. The front door was open, and he walked in. Greg and his forensics team were dusting everything. "Hi, Greg, what's the deal?"

"Hey, Gary. Sorry man. This is a real shit show." He hesitated. "Jenny's upstairs." A clench of the teeth. "I'd go there first. Something happened in the kitchen near the back slider. Lots of stuff going on there. Coroner's been upstairs. She's at the back now."

"Okay Greg, thanks. Anything here?"

"Multiple hits on one set," answered the technician "An old second print but faded."

"Maybe mine from last month." He paused. "Helping her get settled and all. Okay, thanks."

Gary hesitated at the stairs. A half set led to the upper level of the back split and another half set led down to the kitchen. He mounted the stairs to the upper level and found the bathroom. Trevor Harvey, Fred's partner, was there with a forensic tech. Trevor had less than four months as a detective. Inexperienced, but he had to hand it to him, dedicated.

"Hi, Trevor. What do we …" Gary stopped and stared. Jenny lay on the tile floor, her eyes glazed over. The bag had been removed from her head. Someone had at least covered her body up. Gary's knees buckled and he reached for the wall. "Jesus Christ." He took a minute to compose himself. "Okay. Give it to me."

Trevor reached out to Gary's arm. "Gary, I'm sorry."

"That's fine. Jesus. Let's have it."

"Okay, it looks like the perp snuck in and got a plastic bag over her head and dragged her from the tub. Coroner says from the bruising on her neck she was choked from the front. And her head was bashed repeatedly against the tiling." Trevor looked away.

"Bastard."

"The coroner is not sure if she died from asphyxiation or the injury to her skull."

"We got a good DNA sample from under her fingernail," the tech spoke up. "Whoa, are you okay, bud?" he asked.

"I'll be fine," Gary responded, his face ashen. This was harder than he thought.

"She must have fought hard."

"Yeah, that would be her, alright." Gary turned away.

Two worker bees from the coroner's office came into the room. "Can we bag her now?" one of them asked. "You guys done?"

Gary grabbed the guy and shoved him against the wall. "Don't ever talk about her like that again, asshole."

The man put his hands up. "Sorry. I didn't mean any disrespect."

"Well, you need to realize who you're dealing with. It's not just another body." Gary let go of him and looked at Trevor. "Anything else?"

The tech closed his case. "I'm done."

Trevor nodded. "No. You guys can go ahead but take it easy."

Gary left the room and headed downstairs. The kitchen had an eat-in table near the back glass sliding door. In the room were four forensic techs collecting evidence and dusting for prints. Standing to the side was Fred Winkley. A body lay on the floor on the far side of the table. The coroner was kneeling beside it and stood up.

"Three gunshots wounds in his left side. Close range. Maybe right against the body. Ninety percent sure that's what killed him. I'll know more after the autopsy. This is up your alley, but I suspect the killer was laying under him when he took the shots. Times of deaths are between 12:30 and 1:30. Let the boys know when they can take the body."

"T-thanks." Fred said. He looked at Gary. "S-sorry, Gary."

"Hi, Fred. Yeah, it's a bugger all right. That's her ex. What're your thoughts?"

"N-not sure if he d-done Jenny then got wacked or his killer did them b-both."

A uniformed policeman called from the sliding door. "Detective Winkley, several neighbours woke up from what sounded like a single gunshot. A couple of minutes later they heard three more. They saw a man fleeing the house. He was described as average build. He got into a car, dark, SUV, and drove west down the street. One person caught the license plate as GHL something. Another was sure it was OLI 3 something. Another thought he might have seen the car parked here before. There's another car parked down the street registered to a Mark Downey. Neighbours say it's not from around here. I've got all their phone numbers and addresses."

"T-thanks Officer. I'll see them later today."

"Sirs." It was one of the forensic techs. "Got a few flowerpots lined up on the counter here. Looks like one's missing. Lots of ceramic pieces around the body. With all this dirt scattered around maybe the guy who did the shooting got beaned…"

"Yeah, maybe," said Gary.

"But the curious thing is this here shard has a lot of blood on it. There are no cuts on this guy's face or arms." He flicked a thumb towards the body. "See how this edge has blood on it almost a quarter inch. Your guy that got away could have a significant cut somewhere. May even need an ER visit. We'll run DNA, od course. We also found this cell phone under the victim's body. It's code locked."

"Thanks," muttered Fred.

"We'll need another hour or so here."

"Ok-kay." Fred looked at the uniformed policeman. "Have the hospitals c-checked." The officer nodded and left.

"I'm going to have a look around," said Gary. "Okay, Fred?"

"W… whatever," Fred sneered.

Gary chose not to respond and wandered around the kitchen. He stopped by the sliding door. Glass fragments outside. Nothing inside. They hadn't broken the window to gain entry. Either they had a key, or they picked the lock. He examined the lock. Easy enough to pick. Have to wait and see if dead Mark over there had any picks on him. Did the glass get blown out by a stray bullet? Next, he checked the stove and dishwasher. No activity here. No late snacks or expected visitors. All the wine bottles were corked. He walked up the stairs to the living room. Same thing. No signs of a guest or late visitor. What was Mark doing here at midnight? Jenny wouldn't have had him over. She never mentioned the fact she was meeting him when she left work. Forced entry? Maybe he came to have words and it escalated. No. Not with the plastic bag. That rang as premeditated. A cowardly, sneak attack.

And who was the guy that shot Mark? What was their involvement? Three shots to the body. Louis came to mind. That threatening gesture in the courtroom. Did he have one of his flunkeys try to do her in? *They should have put a detail on her.*

Gary sank into one of the chairs. His eyes moistened and a tear streamed down his cheek. Poor Jenny. He would miss her. She was good people. Her dogged determination, great sense for sniffing out clues, snappy attitude, and relentless dedication to her job, were all qualities he loved about her. *We could have used you on this one, Jenny.*

He needed to get out of here. Gary stood. Not much more he could do. He'd have to wait until all the forensics came in, ballistic reports, autopsies. Then he could sniff around a bit and make sure Fred was doing okay by her. He knew he would; Fred was a great detective, a little standoffish at times, but knew his stuff. Gary often wondered if he seemed that way because of his stutter.

Captain Dan Ridley was still outside when Gary left the front door.

"No fistfights, I see."

"No," Gary responded. "I laid on all the self-control I could muster."

"Good, Now let him be and no more prying. I want this solved as well as you, but I don't need a turf war on my hands. You have enough to do. Is that clear?"

"Clear as a bell."

"Good. Now go home. Take today off, and tomorrow as well."

"Okay, Cappy."

Gary walked to his car and drove away, planning how he could work his way into the investigation.

***

Fred Winkley stood staring into space. What a shitstorm. If the guy who shot ol' Mark here was who he thought it was, and that cell phone belonged to him, Fred could be in a lot of trouble. It was bagged and tagged and recorded, so he couldn't make it go missing. At least he was lead on the investigation. He'd have to keep Gary away and control that Trevor partner of his. Shit. You pay good money to have a job done and it goes to shit. At least the money wasn't his own. *Gotta love the evidence locker.* He smiled for the second time that night. The first was when he'd heard of Jenny's murder.

***

Four days later Fred was reading some of the reports: autopsy, forensics, and ballistics. The Computer Investigation Forensics Technicians, CIFT, were still working their magic on the red phone. DNA under Jenny's fingernails matched that of her ex, Mark Downey. So, he had done the deed. She suffered significant trauma to the back of her head but died of asphyxiation due to a crushed windpipe. The coroner was releasing the body tomorrow. He supposed he'd have to attend the funeral.

Ballistics identified the rounds embedded in Mark as .38's. They appeared to be self-loaded with extra gunpowder for higher velocity. The points had been filed with an X for maximum destruction. They had ricocheted around the chest cavity, tearing organs apart. Nobody walked away from these rounds. Definitely a pro. Likely his man. He had paid good money to that Gryphon fellow, but Mark was the one who had done it.

Blood from the ceramic shard indicated different blood than Mark's. There was no DNA hit on the second blood sample, another good thing. Maybe his man could lay low, and this would pass.

On the other hand, forensics had found a shoe print at the side of the house not matching Mark's, another possible nail for Fred's coffin. Overall, it wasn't too bad. Jenny's murder was solved and that would alleviate a lot of pressure. Some might even hail Mark's killer as a bit of a hero for getting rid of him.

Fred spent the next hour typing up his report on Jenny's murder, humming a tune.

***

The next day, Gary was going over the report on Jenny's murder, courtesy of the Cappy. So, Mark had done it. Not Louis, or a minion of his. But who was the person that offed Mark? Was he tied to Louis at all? Gary strolled over to the captain's office and knocked on the door frame.

"Come in."

Gary walked in. "Cappy, I've been thinking about the second guy at Jenny's house."

"Well, don't. You've got other cases. Clean them up."

"Yeah, I'm keeping my distance, but another head might help. That Trevor fellow is only worth half a head. He's so green he's still sucking lollipops."

"Kojak sucked lollipops."

"Okay, fine. But still, maybe I can help. A fresh set of eyes and all. Through you. I won't talk to Fred directly. Can't anyways. Can't deal with that stutter."

Dan rubbed his forehead. "Okay. Here's the password for the mystery killer reports. Fred thinks it's a dead-end, though."

***

Gryphon watched the blond bimbo on the news reporting about the police sergeant murdered in her own home. Her ex, Mark Downey, had killed her but there were additional circumstances the police were looking into. She went on to describe the man and the vehicle they were looking for, emphasizing each detail with the tap of her fingernail.

Gryphon thought about the situation, sipping on a brandy. His biggest problem would be that insufferable Two-Toes Louis. The man would want his money back. Gryphon was not troubled by the police. They had protocols to follow. He was more concerned about the underhanded methods Louis would employ to find and exact a refund.

But first things first. His wound was healing. It was time to get rid of the car. Tomorrow he would look after it. He poured another brandy.

The next morning found him eyeing the RAV. He'd dismantled the GPS five years ago when he acquired the car. It had sat here for a year until he had registered it to a dead man. He eased himself in the car, the plates already removed and backed out of the garage. A trail around the side of his house led to the woods on his property. There were so many trails leading onto Crown land, and he was soon deep into the woods.

He found an open area, grassy, and away from any trees. He spread the naphtha evenly over the car. Serial numbers and VIN had been removed in the garage. He lit the trail of naphtha leading to the car and it caught fire with a 'woomfth'. The car was ablaze instantly and when he was satisfied with its progress, Gryphon left the smoldering wreck and walked home. He took his time.

It allowed him to think about his next move.

***

The aroma of fresh coffee filled the detectives' office the next morning. Trevor was squirming like a little child, ready for some action. Fred was not as eager. His thoughts went to the cell phone. It could become problematic. So could his partner. He needed to slow him down, some.

"It's g-gonna be a tough one, Trev. Looks like this g-guy is a pro. CIFT can't c-crack the cell phone. We don't have a license number to run. Not much of a d-description either. This will probably drag on to a c-cold case."

"Well, we can't give up that easily. I had DMV run some sort of algorithm with the info we gave them. Maybe something will turn up."

"Yeah, maybe." Fred hoped not. *Let this settle for a bit and we can just cruise. Make it look like we're working the case. Something else will come in and this will go to the back burner.* His computer dinged. A new email.

"Oh, what's that?" his overenthusiastic partner asked.

"Let me check." Fred opened the e-mail. It was a message from CIFT.

Fred, we were able to crack the phone, and attached are the numbers called and received. No pictures, yet. GPS was turned off, but we might have a workaround for that. We're trying to recover some deleted texts. I'll keep you posted. Jerry.

Fred's eyes darted to Trevor, back to the email, then around the office. Trevor looked at him. Fred waved him off.

"Nothing much. Something from HR. Pension shit."

"Oh. Yeah. Okay." Trevor sat back in his seat.

No one else was looking. He opened the attachment. Right there, the first number, from eleven days ago, that damned cell phone he'd bought. His call to Gryphon. *So, it was him in the house. Jesus, what a shit show. Wait. Deleted texts? Had that bugger recorded him? Was his voice recorded on the phone?*

Bile climbed up his esophagus as he fought to maintain control.

"You don't look too good, Fred. Everything okay?"

"Ummm, yeah. Uhh. Yeah, everything is f-fine." Fred closed the attachment then deleted the email. Then he went into the deleted folder and permanently deleted it. "Look Trev, something came up that I g-gotta deal with. I'll be gone this afternoon. Why don't you t-take off, too? We'll start fresh, Monday."

"Okay, Fred. Hope everything is okay. I'm going to stay for a bit. Taking my girl out for lunch. Then I'll book out."

"Yeah, yeah, whatever." Fred barely heard what Trevor said as he was standing to go. "Bye." He rushed out the side door and headed to his car.

Twenty minutes later he was at home and found the cell phone. He tore the battery out, then fumbled with the SIM card, snapped it in two. He stomped on the cell phone several times.

He left his house with all three pieces and headed away from downtown. At Devon Park, he tossed the battery in a trash can. Then he drove to High Park and got rid of the SIM card. He continued his drive and stopped halfway over the Stappleton Bridge. Traffic was light and he tossed the phone into the river, unseen.

He spent the rest of the afternoon and well into the night in a bar he'd never been to before.

***

Trevor shut down his computer and grabbed his suit jacket. He checked his tie and ran fingers through his hair. Time for lunch. He took the stairs to the basement. The evidence locker was down here and the computer forensic techs hung out in the far corner. One of the techs was Allie Fortin, Trevor's girlfriend. She was waiting for him to go to lunch.

"Hey there. How's your day going?" she asked.

"Not bad. Kinda stuck on the Downey murder. Mark, that is."

"Yeah, well maybe the phone list will help."

"What phone list?" Trevor scrunched his nose.

"The one we got off the cell phone. We sent it to Fred."

"Oh," Trevor creased his brow. "He didn't say anything. He got a message that kinda messed him up. Maybe family or something. Tore on outta here."

"Oh. Hope he's okay. Anyway, I've got a hard copy. You can get it when we get back." She grabbed his arm. "Where we going for lunch?"

"Hmmm. Sushi, or Italian?"

"Sushi. I'll fall asleep if I load up on carbs."

"Sushi it is."

After lunch, Trevor sat at his desk checking out the list of phone numbers. He was about to put in the request to trace the numbers on the list when the phone rang.

"Hello, Detective Harvey."

"Hi, sweetheart. How are you?"

"Fine, Mom." Trevor rolled his eyes. "What's up?"

"Well, I was just wondering how my favorite son is doing?"

"I'm your only son, remember, and I'm doing fine."

"Yes, I know, dear. That's why you're my favorite. Could you do me a favor?"

"Possibly. What is it?"

"I have an ophthalmologist appointment this afternoon. They're going to put those dreadful drops in. I can't possibly drive myself home. Daddy was supposed to drive, but he's in one of his moods, you know, and I'd prefer if you took me."

Trevor glanced around. The captain was out. Fred did tell him to shut it down. It was close to three on a Friday. The phone list could wait until Monday. "Okay, Mom. I'm on my way."

"That's a dear."

Trevor hung up and locked the list in his desk drawer. He made his way out the side entrance to the parking lot.

***

Gary logged into the Mark Downey file to check for any new information. Nothing. Was Fred dragging his heels? Gary decided to spend part of the weekend scoping out Louis 'Two Toes' Lefebvre.

The next morning, he spent two uneventful hours at Louis's club. Nothing of interest happening here. Time to pack it in and take the kids to the park. Maybe he would hassle Trevor for some information on Monday.

***

Monday morning bright and early found Trevor at his desk. He'd placed his request to trace the numbers on the list and was waiting back, although he was told it might take a day or so. He had the file opened and was about to enter the list as part of the investigation when Fred rolled in. He was red-eyed and looked like shit.

"Holy crap, Fred. Are you all right?"

"Yeah, yeah, I'll spruce up in a b-bit. Never mind me. What are you up to?"

"Hey, say, listen. I got a …" Trevor's phone rang. "Just a sec." He held his finger up to Fred. "Hello, Detective Harvey."

"Hello, this is Francine from the DMV. We have a possible hit on that Rav4. License number GLE 347, 2014, blue. Registered to a John Anders, 123 Landover Crescent."

"Okay." Trevor grabbed a pen. "Give me that again… John Anders… 123 Landover Crescent. Great. Thanks." He slammed down the receiver. "Hey, Fred. Got a hit on the suspect's car, and an address. We're thinking he's a pro, should we call SWAT?"

***

Fred's stomach swirled. He popped some Tums and silently swore. It would be better to bring SWAT in. Maybe this Gryphon guy would get killed in the raid. Silence him forever. "Yeah, sounds g-good, Trev. Make it happen." Trevor got on the phone as Fred swallowed another four Tums. He wasn't sure he'd make it through the raid, either. He bounded up and raced to the washroom. He deposited breakfast and most of the rum from the night before. After he stopped dry heaving, he cleaned himself, swearing he'd never drink again.

Fred trudged back to his desk. Trevor looked up. "It's all set up, Fred. We meet SWAT in two hours at Highland Park, two blocks away from the perp. I'm off to pick up the warrant now."

"Good. I'll wait here." He burped. Something horrible wafted out.

***

Lieutenant Jerry King from the SWAT unit conferred with Trevor and Fred. They were at Highland Park and checking their kit.

"We deployed a plainclothesman. He saw some movement in what he figures is the living room. One person. How do you want to handle this?" he asked Fred. "You have control until I see a tactical threat."

Fred inwardly sighed. He wanted a barn-storming assault, but it would look suspicious and could backfire on him. "Okay, this guy is a p-pro. Consider any unusual movement on his behalf as d-dangerous. Trevor and I will knock on the door. If he doesn't answer b-break the door down and move in. If he opens the d-door, move in and t-take him down."

"Aah, detective. No can do. I can't barge in unless there's a threat. You talk to him and determine the situation. I'll have two teams at the back as well. You notice anything unusual, let me know. If any action starts, stay out of our way. Are we good here?"

Fred nodded

Jerry walked away, twirling his finger. His squad jumped into action. Ten minutes later they were deployed around 123 Landover Crescent.

Trevor and Fred sauntered up to the front door and knocked. "Mr. Anders?" Trevor called out. They heard some shuffling inside. S.W.A.T. members were tucked out of sight on either side of the door.

Fred shushed him. "Anders c-could be an alias, you idiot," Fred whispered. "You want to s-spook him?"

Trevor cringed as the latch on the door clicked. The door opened a crack; a thin man stood there. He wore a white shirt with a knitted cardigan over it and wrinkled blue jeans.

"What do you want? I don't do charities. Go away."

"Sir, I'm d-detective Fred Winkley. I have a f-few…"

"I told you I don't do charities." The man reached into his cardigan pocket where Fred noticed a bulge. The man began to close the door.

"Gun!" called Fred.

Two S.W.A.T members barged in knocking the man down. "On the floor. Hands where we can see them."

The man on the floor began screaming. "My hip. My hip. Aaaah. It's killing me. I think it's broke." One of the men cuffed his hands behind his back. Two others entered over the man and began a sweep of the house.

"Sir, are there any others in the house?"

"Aaaarrgh. God, it hurts. Stop moving me. No, there's no one else. What are you doing? Who are you people?"

"Police. What's your name, sir?"

"Alex McInnis. Why are you here? I've done nothing wrong. You've gone and broken my hip."

Jerry motioned for Fred and Trevor to come in. Fred looked at the man. Maybe seventy, thin, arthritic hands, not much of a contract killer. A TV remote lay beside him. "Trev, send for the b-bus. Possible f-fracture of the hip." He bent over the man. "Sir we have an ambulance c-coming. Is this your house?"

"Yes. Why do you care? What are you doing here? I haven't done anything."

"When did you purchase it?"

"Aaa." The man was grasping his hip, writhing.

"Do you know a John Anders?"

"No, I don't. You're gonna hear from my lawyer. I served in Nam, you know."

A crowd was gathering outside. A local news van pulled up and a reporter with a camerawoman began filming. Some of the neighbours were soon interviewed. The ambulance arrived and took the older gentleman away. He was cursing the police all the way to the street. The news team got a good shot of him yelling about police brutality and invasion of privacy.

Fred called forensics to come and sweep the house, but he figured they had the wrong guy.

"Hey Fred. Here's his driver's license. Says Alex McInnis. Born 1948. Sure looks like him." Fred took the license. *Yeah, it sure did look like him. What a mess.*

"Put a uni on his hospital room until we verify all this."

Fred felt a wave of relief. This was not their man. It let him off the hook but created a whole other PR shitstorm.

He needed to stop by the drugstore and get some Pepto.

Trevor and Fred were sitting in the captain's office, squirming.

"What happened?" demanded the captain.

"We got a hit on a p-possible address for the suspect," Fred said. "We r-reacted."

"Yes, you certainly did. SWAT! What the hell? Did you have any corroborating evidence before storming Fort Knox?"

"Not really, sir," Trevor spoke.

Dan pointed a finger at him. "You shut up!" He glared at Fred. "Our 'dangerous criminal' is still in surgery, and I've already got a call from an attorney. What a mess. This greenhorn has an excuse. You know better."

"I'm not a greenhorn, sir."

"What part of shut up don't you understand?" Dan yelled without taking his eyes off the senior detective. "Fred, what's up with you?"

"I don't know, Captain. Maybe it's J-Jenny and all. Just want to g-get this bugger."

"Yeah, we all do. Well, you've left a big mess. The chief is breathing down my neck. You should be on administrative leave, but I'm short detectives as it is. You're still working but on a short leash. Watch your step. Any storming of castles goes through me. Got it?"

"Y-yes, Captain."

They stood and left the office.

"Sorry if I got you in trouble." Trevor stood at his desk.

Fred threw up his hands. "It's okay. N-never mind. Look, I'm going for a d-drink. Alone. You c-can stay here if you want. Do whatever." Fred headed for the door.

Gary found Trevor was sitting at his desk. He placed his hand on Trevor's shoulder. "I hear you were involved in a bit of a row."

Trevor looked up at him. "Yeah. The captain's not too happy."

"So where did you get that address from?"

"DMV. I have the VIN, year, and such."

"Can I see it?" Trevor handed him the papers. "Did you try tracking the vehicle's GPS to find out its location?"

"No, not yet. Fred didn't seem too interested in pursuing that."

"I have some contacts that may be able to help. Want me to try?" Gary offered.

"Sure." Trevor shrugged. "Go ahead. I think I'm heading home."

"Yeah, take it easy. And don't worry about the captain. It'll all blow over." Trevor grimaced. "Hey." Gary waved the papers. "Keep this between the two of us, okay."

"Sure thing."

Gary left Trevor sprawled in his chair, head lowered, with hands wiping his face, and walked back to his station. He checked his contacts and dialed a number. "Hey there, Jeff. It's Gary Johnson from the police department."

"Hey Gary. What's up?"

"I've got a VIN." He read it off. "Can you trace the GPS on it? It's involved in a homicide."

"Sure, let me check." There were a series of keyboard clicks, then some silence. "Hey Gary. No present location. The GPS must have been removed or disabled. That's not so easy. Your fellow knows what he's doing."

"Shit, so you don't know the last location or anything?"

"Hang on, not all is lost. What is this… a 2014. Let me check a couple of things and I'll call you back tomorrow, the day after at the latest."

"Thanks, Jeff. I owe you."

"You owe me many. I'll be in touch. Bye."

"Bye."

***

Gryphon heard the news about the SWAT assault on the old man. He chuckled as he visualized the chewing out the cops were getting, although he sympathized with the old man. He was glad he disposed of the car. One less thing to worry about.

But there was another problem.

Right now, he was listening to a recording from Louis's office, courtesy of a bug he had planted when he was there.

"Bobby, it just ain't right." It was Louis Lefebvre talking. Bobby Simpson was his side-kick lieutenant as Gryphon recalled. "That fucker took my money and didn't do the job. He owes me."

"We'll never find him, Louis. He's disappeared."

"I have methods. We'll find him. Listen. Go get that kid that helped us with the dark web contacts. I'm gonna employ him again."

"Sure thing, Louis."

Gryphon stopped the recording. This Louis fellow was becoming a pain in the ass. He'd have to do something about that. Gryphon poured a brandy as he began a preliminary search for places to escape to.

It might be time for a change.

***

The next morning, Trevor started going through the list of numbers from the cell phone, when he got an e-mail listing where all the SIM cards from the red phone list had been purchased. The first one on the list had been purchased at a kiosk in a local mall. He phoned the kiosk but there was no answer. *Probably not there yet.* Trevor wondered whether he should wait for Fred. He looked around. Gary wasn't in either. He decided to drive to the mall and check out the kiosk. He left a note for his partner.

The mall was small in terms of malls; a Bay at one end and thirty to forty stores with a food court at the junction of the "T". Trevor addressed the map, then made his way to the kiosk near the end of one of the crosses in the T. It offered cell phones, plans from a dozen providers, and repairs. He flashed his badge.

"You sold a SIM card with this number," he said handing a piece of paper to the young man behind the counter, "and I need to know who bought it."

"Well, uh, I, uh… I should probably phone my boss."

"Listen. I don't have time to wait around." Trevor leaned in. "Don't make this hard for me, or you. All I want is a name."

"Uh..."

"If I have to come back with a warrant, I won't be happy."

"Okay. When was it again?"

"Sometime before 6:30 PM on the 22 June."

The kid looked through the computer, then pulled out some binders. "Here it is," he stated. "On the 18th."

"What's the name?"

"Uh, there isn't one."

"What do you mean there isn't one? You sold it to someone. There has to be a name and address and credit card number."

"They must have paid cash."

"Okay, so give me the address."

"It's not there."

"What do you mean it's not there? You sold a SIM card to someone without getting any information?"

"Not me. It was probably Johnny. Look, officer, or captain. Sometimes if the extra cash is enough, Johnny will sell things and 'forget' to collect the information. You know, like, we get minimum wage here and all."

Shit. What was he going to do now? Trevor arched his head back and grimaced. He spotted a mall security camera near the entrance, pointing toward the kiosk. He smiled. "Can you at least tell me when this transaction took place?"

"Umm, okay, let me see. It was the third one. The first one was a credit card at 9:12. We open at 9:00. The next was cash. The fourth one was at 10:27 by debit, so between 9:12 and 10:27." The kid looked up smiling.

"Where's the administration office?"

"Down near the food court."

"Stop taking money under the table." Trevor glared at him before turning and walking to the administration office.

***

Gary was reading a report when his phone rang.

"Hello, Detective Johnson."

"Gary, old buddy. It's Jeff. Got some good news for you."

"Yeah, what? You getting divorced?"

"No, not that good. But I got the last location for your friend."

Gary copied the address. "Thanks, Jeff. That's out in the boonies, right?"

"I Google Earthed it. Yeah, you're right. Nice digs. You going after the big fish, now?"

"Yeah, maybe," he said as he fired up the program. "Thanks a lot, Jeff."

He entered the address and waited as it zoomed in on the property. It *was* in the boonies. Surrounded by open area. It would be hard to move in unnoticed. He'd have to do a bit more research before taking it to the captain.

Where was Fred, or Trevor, for that matter?

***

After flashing his badge a couple of times, Trevor ended up in a small room with a security guard.

"We have them sorted in folders by day, then by camera. When was it again?" Trevor told him and he clicked the right folder. "Here you go. I'll fast forward to 9:00 AM."

"It's the third guy that buys something." Trevor leaned in. The image ran through the first and second purchaser, then a third showed up at the kiosk. "There. Play that." They watched as a woman dropped off a cell phone.

"Doesn't look like a purchase to me," the guard offered.

"Yeah." Trevor agreed. "Next person." Soon a man in a suit strolled up to the counter. Something about the guy seemed familiar to Trevor. The man glanced around, then leaned over the counter and it looked like he flashed some money at the salesperson. The salesperson nodded. He pocketed the money. The image was clear enough. "Okay. I need a good shot of the guy doing the purchase." Just then the man looked in the direction of the camera. "There! That's it. Stop it." The guard stopped it and backed up frame by frame, zoomed-in until the face filled the screen. The image left no doubt of the identity of the man purchasing the SIM card. It was his partner, Fred Winkley.

Trevor flopped into a chair. His stomach churned and he felt light-headed.

"Are you all right, sir?"

Trevor waved him away. "Can you print that? Better yet, can you save it?"

"Yep, I'll save this and copy the whole folder to a USB for you. Is this the guy you're looking for?"

"It is, but not who I expected."

"Do you know this guy?"

"Can't say. It's part of an ongoing investigation. But you've helped immensely." Trevor took the offered USB and then stopped. "Can you email that picture to someone?"

"Sure thing. Who to?"

"Can I type it?" The guard nodded as he opened the office email. Trevor sat in the chair and typed Allie's work email. He attached the photo, explained what he found, and told her to take this to either Gary Johnson or the captain.

"Thanks a million, buddy." He offered his hand to the guard. He hurried out the office and to his car. He phoned Gary's office number but there was no answer. He didn't know the detective's cell number.

***

Allie was working on cracking a hard drive code when her computer dinged and a small window came up stating a new email from Pineridge Mall Administration, subject: LOOK AT THIS. She shook her head. The spam was even getting through to the department mail. She dismissed the notice and went back to work.

***

Fred Winkley arrived at his desk around 11:00 that morning. His head throbbed from another night staring into a bottle. Maybe today would be better. He plunked into his chair and looked at the mess on his desk. There was a note from Trevor.

Gone to Pineridge Mall to track down the first number on the list. Could be important. See you when I get back.

What number? What list? Pineridge Mall. Oh, shit. Butterflies began a cursory exploration of his stomach. He looked over at Trevor's desk. Laying on top of his "in" basket was a familiar-looking list. *Where did he get that?* Fred looked at it and yes, there was the number, his number, at the top. *That little no-good Dudley Do-right.* Wait. He'd paid cash. There was no trace. He'd even bribed the kid to forget about his name and address. Trever would find nothing. He sat down and mopped his brow.

Cameras. Mall cameras. Were there any? He couldn't remember. *Shit.* The butterflies were in full flight now, performing a Snow Birds routine. Bile was gurgling up his throat. He chugged some Pepto as he thought about how to play this.

Fred grabbed some plastic ties from his desk. He drew his gun and checked the rounds and action. He'd only fired his gun once in his career.

Today may be his second.

A few minutes later, he was sitting in his car watching for Trevor. The camera outside the door focussed on the entrance and he had no fear of being seen out this far. When the kid arrived, he would know by his body language he had found something. Then he would take the appropriate action.

***

Trevor backed into a parking spot at the police station. He was gathering his things when a car pulled up beside him on the driver's side. Someone got out and stood by his door. Trevor took his time putting his phone away and let the person move between the cars. When he saw no movement, he glanced around to see who was there.

***

Fred saw the panic in Trevor's eyes as his young partner fumbled for his phone, then his gun. Fred tapped on the window with *his* gun, shielding it from view by others in the parking lot, and made a winding motion, while shaking his head. The window wound down.

"Don't t-try anything funny, Trev. Put your hands on the s-steering wheel. That's it. Okay," Fred placed his gun against Trevor's temple. "Hold still now. I'm g-gonna reach in and get your g-gun," Fred pulled the gun from the holster on Trevor's left side and placed it in his pocket. "Where's your phone?"

"Fred, you don't have to do this. We can work something out."

"The phone!"

"In my inside jacket pocket."

"Slowly get it out. N-no funny business." Trevor handed the phone to Fred. "Okay, left hand up here on that g-grab handle." Fred extracted a zip tie and managed to secure Trevor's hand. His arm dangled from the handle. "Don't move." Fred scrambled around to the passenger door and got in. He attached another zip tie to the wheel, fumbling a bit with his one hand, leaving a little slack. He looped a second tie through and ordered Trevor to slip his hand through. Then he tightened it. "There, that should do. Start the car and drive to Blenham Park."

"What?"

"I said drive to Blenham Park. Outside the city."

"Yeah, I know where it is. What for?"

"Use your imagination. Now get going."

***

Allie locked the hard drive in her desk and went to clear her emails. Section meeting this Friday, a reminder of security protocols, and here was that spam from the mall. She read the subject LOOK AT THIS and was about to delete it when something caught her eye. The first line read: *Allie, it's Trevor. This...*The rest was hidden. She opened the email and read the complete message, then opened the attachment. A muscle at her jaw-line quivered as she pieced together the significance of this. She printed the email and attached picture, then saved a copy of the email on her personal drive, logged out, grabbed the printouts and her purse, and headed out to find the captain.

Upstairs, Fred was not around. The captain's door was closed, and she could see the lights were out. Gary was at his desk looking at his computer. She grabbed a chair and rolled it over.

"You need to look at this." She shoved the papers in his face. He looked at her quizzically. She explained about sending the list of phone numbers to Fred, then giving Trevor a copy.

"When was that?"

"Last Friday."

Gary thought for a minute. "Can you check Fred's email?"

"Sure, let me log in." She worked the keyboard and two minutes later pointed to the screen. "There. He deleted it three minutes after he received it. No print request either."

"Damn it! Where's Trevor now?" Worry crept into Gary's voice. Allie threw up her hands.

"I got this around 11:30. Said he was coming right back."

Gary checked for Fred. Not around. On his desk were Trevor's list and the note Trever had left him. He looked at his watch. It was 12:55.

They ran out the side door.

"There's Fred's car. Do you see Trevor's?"

"No. He should be back by now." She clenched her hands and breathed heavily. "Where is he? What do we do now?"

Gary placed his hands on her shoulders. "Okay, calm down. I'll call his cell."

"Here, I can do that." She pulled out her phone and dialed, stepping from one foot to the other while it went to voice mail. "Trevor, it's Allie. Phone me as soon as you get this." She closed her phone. "No answer."

"Okay." Gary held the door for her. "Let's head inside."

Back inside, Gary asked another detective if he'd seen Fred.

"Oh, about an hour and a half ago, maybe two. I saw him grabbing some plastic ties and checking his gun. Figured he was meeting Trev for some sort of bust. Maybe they got another lead or something."

"Thanks, Tommy." Gary saw that the captain was back and led Allie in there.

"We got a big problem Cappy."

"How so?"

"Last Friday Fred received an email from CIFT about a list of numbers from that red phone found at Jenny's.

"The one we think belonged to the guy that got away?"

"Yeah, that's it…"

"But then he deleted it," Allie butt in. "Then I gave Trevor a copy and he checked them out and found out it was Fred who made the last phone call, and Fred found out that Trevor found out, and now Fred has Trevor and he's going to kill him."

Captain Dan Ridley twisted his head. "What?"

Gary placed his hand in front of Allie. He looked at his captain. "Fred received the email, then deleted it. He must have deleted it because the last number to call the red phone belonged to him. It was a secondary, burner number. Meanwhile, Trevor got a copy of the phone numbers from Allie, here, and investigated the first number. Turns out it was Fred. He emailed this picture," Gary showed the printout to the captain showing Fred buying the card, "to Allie before lunch, and now he's gone missing. Fred's car is here but Trevor's is gone. So, I'm thinking Fred may have Trevor in Trevor's car."

"And Fred going to kill him." Allie was shifting feet again. "We have to do something."

Dan placed the photo on his desk. "Put a BOLO (Be On Look Out) out on Trevor's vehicle. I'll request a GPS location. Fred! God damn it. What a shit show."

Gary and Allie left the office and Allie slapped her head. "Duh. I've got the Find My app for Trevor's phone." She fumbled with hers until she had a location. "Looks like outside the city. Umm, it says, Blenham Park, I think." She expanded the screen. "Yeah, Blenham Park."

Gary stuck his head in the captain's office. "We have a location for Trevor's phone. Blenham Park."

"Blenham Park. That's more a forest preserve than a park," observed the captain.

"Here are the coordinates." Allie rattled off some numbers.

"Go," commanded Dan. "Take Tommy. And be careful." He looked at Allie. "Sorry, you're not going. Too dangerous."

"But I have to go. Besides, I have the coordinates." She glanced at her phone. "Looks like they're moving, too."

Dan shook his head. "Nope. Not a chance. Give Gary the information for that app. You can stay right here in my office." To Gary he said. "I'll get unis there for backup. And the canine team."

Gary grabbed Tommy and the two of them headed out to the parking lot.

***

Blenham Park was not considered a park anymore. It used to serve as a picnic area with a large open grassy area for Frisbee and pick-up football.

Surrounding the grassy area on three sides was one fifty acres of woods with interconnecting trails, rarely used. City attractions like the wave pool, waterslides, mini-putt, and escape rooms all drew visitors away from nature. Funding dwindled as well as interest and the park became neglected and was mostly abandoned.

It was with this in mind that Fred guided Trevor along an overrun trail deep into the forest, with the young detective's wrists tied behind him.

"You don't have to do this, Fred," Trevor pleaded over his shoulder. His hands were secured behind him.

"S-shut up."

"Look, take my car and go."

"S-shut up, I said. Ok-kay, this is far enough. Over by that t-tree." He motioned with his gun. "That's it, now stay p-put." Fred holstered his gun and brought out Trevor's. "It's g-gonna be a suicide. C-couldn't handle the pressure." Fred moved to Trevor's right side. "D-don't move a muscle." He placed the gun against Trevor's temple. After his partner was dead, he planned to fire another shot with the gun in Trevor's hand, so there would be powder residue on his hand.

Trevor went to speak and Fred shut him up. "You had to go m-meddling. C-couldn't leave it alone."

Fred pulled the trigger.

***

Gryphon had decided it was time to go. He had shut down his business, closed his other apartment, and was preparing to destroy this house. There had always been an exit strategy and now was the time. He finished with the last of the incendiary devices and secured it in the garage. Dozens of other such devices were spread around the house, connected to a detonator, as well as liters of gas and white phosphorus in his secret room. There would be nothing of significance left after the fires.

He took a last look around and shrugged his shoulders. It had been a good run here, but it was time to move on. His overnight bag got tossed in the back seat of one of his cars, and he nestled an additional package beside it. He had three sets of documents with him and four more had been forwarded to an address in Europe.

The garage door opened, and he backed out, drove down the lane, and buzzed the gate open for the last time. He took his time driving downtown near the train station and found a twenty-four-hour parking garage. He bought the two-day option and parked on the upper level, near the elevator.

A Fed-Ex office was two blocks away and he negotiated for the package to be delivered on Monday morning; five days from today. It was addressed to the 5th Division Police Building, attention Detective Gary Johnson. Gryphon chuckled at the thought of what would happen when it was opened. It would rock that building to the core.

He hailed a taxi and directed them to the airport. Gryphon was flying to Toronto, then Chicago where he would stay tonight.

***

Gary pulled into Blenham park in record time. Trevor's car was there. Tommy and he jumped out of the car. He brought up the app on his phone. It indicated a spot 800 meters down a trail.

Tommy had checked Trevor's car and shook his head. "Not much. Plastic straps on the steering wheel. I think he's got him."

"Okay. We need to be extra careful, then."

Three police cars pulled into the parking lot. Four officers jumped out of the vehicles. One of them called out. "The canine unit should be here shortly. What's the deal?"

"The possible perp is one of us," Gary briefly explained the situation.

They were deciding whether to wait for the canine unit when a muffled shot rang out.

***

Trevor saw Fred switch guns for his. He had been thinking of ways out of this but they all seemed like slim chances. The suicide thing was his only chance. Fred would be close to him and he might be able to do something. He felt the muzzle against his right temple and tensed. He barely heard Fred's stammering as the trigger was squeezed.

Click!

He charged sideways, knocking Fred over, stumbling himself. He reeled but caught himself after several steps. Spinning around, he realized he was too far away and Fred was regaining his feet. Trevor turned and ran down the trail. If he could only get around a corner in the trail. He was faster than Fred for sure, but his hands behind the back hindered his balance. A shot rang out and a twig exploded beside his head. That tubby old bugger was faster than he thought.

Trever stumbled on a root and almost went flying to the ground. He crashed into a tree face first and pain exploded from his broken nose. His eyes watered as he rolled off the path and struggled to regain his feet. Although he could barely see, he *heard* the thumping of Fred's footsteps. He leapt into the brush and tried to make a decent pace while remaining silent.

Another shot and bark flew from a nearby tree. He veered to the left and slid down a small hill. Ahead was a thicket of Sumac and he wormed his way into the center. Trevor thought back to the only thing that had saved him. As many times as he had been told to always have a round chambered, he never did. His theory was he could cock a weapon whenever the need arose. Better that than have an accidental discharge. There had been no round in the chamber when Fred pulled the trigger.

But a lot of good that would do him if he didn't get out of here. He needed to get these plastic ties off of his wrists. Trevor sat down and wiggled his arms down towards his butt. If he could only get them past his butt, he could wriggle his legs through and he'd have his hands in front. Maybe then he could chew on the ties. They dug into his wrists. He arched his back and began to squirm. Blood poured out his nose onto his suit. He heard some movement near the exterior of the thicket. Damn. His left arm slid past his butt cheek, but the right stayed stubbornly behind. Now his arms were stuck and cramping up.

The rustling came closer.

***

They were around 300 meters from Trevor, according to the Find My app, when the second gunshot was heard. Gary had sent the unis down some parallel paths as he and Tommy took the direct route. This time the sound came from their left, off this trail. They headed into the bush.

***

Fred spotted a flash of dark blue and took a quick shot. Missed. Damn it. He spotted the scuff marks where Trevor had slid down this hill. That fucker was close; time to finish this. He was careful skidding down the hill in his dress shoes. They allowed for no purchase whatsoever. The woods opened up a little and he saw a grove of brush and he eased over to them. He thought he heard some noise near the center and entered the grove. The noise increased and he centered in on it. There. The kid was trying to get his arms from behind him around past his ass. Too far for a good shot. He scrambled forward. Fred took careful aim and fired.

***

Trevor thrashed about trying to get his arm around his butt. Both were agonizingly numb and he was beginning to panic. There was no muscle strength left to pull them back either. It was forward or nothing. He began flailing and bit by bit they edged forward. They were about to be freed when heard a twig snap somewhere behind him. He struggled some more and had his one leg through, then the other. He stood on wobbly legs and ran just as he heard the gunshot and felt the impact, knocking him to the ground. A searing pain ran through his right shoulder blade.

***

Gary heard the third shot and called out for Trevor.

They were near the top of the small hill that Trevor had slid down. Find My had Trevor's position about 80 meters away.

"Over by that thicket." He pointed towards the grove.

Tommy nodded and drew his weapon. "Let's go."

They scurried down the hill and advanced on the Sumac grove, spreading out as they went.

***

Fred heard the yell and spun around. Damn it. Who was up there? Never mind them, finish the kid off first, then he'd deal with them if he had to. He turned around and tried to zero in on where the kid had been. These damn bushes were disorienting. Over there, he thought. He moved forward, swatting small branches aside, cursing under his breath. This was turning into a cluster-fuck.

***

Trevor forced himself up despite the pain. He knew if he didn't move, he'd be dead. He scrambled out of the grove and headed to some tree cover. His vision was foggy, and his breathing labored. He coughed and blood splattered. The ground seemed to be heading uphill and he struggled to walk. Every step became more difficult. Things were blurred. To his left, was a ravine. He descended but lost his footing and stumbled forward. Momentum took over and he fell, rolling downhill. Brush whipped his body until he crashed into a boulder, stopping his descent and breaking his collar bone.

He passed out shortly after.

***

Fred could not figure out where that fucker had disappeared to. He was sure he hit him, but the bastard got away. A trail of flattened ground cover looked promising. And what was this? Yes, a spot of blood. Okay, time to run this sucker down.

"Trevor? Fred?" a voice called out from behind him. He spun around, trying to locate it.

"Trevor?" The voice sounded like it was from the other side of the grove. He thought it might be Gary's voice. Time for a different plan. He wiped Trevor's gun as best he could and threw it as far as possible into the bush. He drew his weapon as Gary came into view.

"Drop it," a voice commanded off to the side. He looked and saw Tommy. *Shit, they've got me.*

"Oh, g-good. You're here." He spoke. "We've been c-chasing one of Lefebvre's men. T-trevor went ahead. I think he may have been s-shot. Come on, Let's go."

"Wait a second." It was Gary. "You mean to tell me you were out here chasing down one of Lefebvre's men? Come on Fred."

"Trev got a t-tip about a meet out here. We c-came out to intercept them, and they t-took off into the woods. We chased them. Trevor went ahead and I heard g-gunshots. Come on. We gotta go."

Gary checked his cell. The signal was right there." He stared at Fred. "Why do you have Trevor's phone?" Fred had no response.

Gary stared at Fred. His story seemed feasible, although knowing what they had uncovered at the division, not likely.

Gary made the decision. "Drop the weapon, Fred. Now."

"You're m-making a mistake. We need to g-go get these guys."

"The weapon! Drop it!"

Fred tossed his gun on the ground.

"Hands behind you."

Fred hesitated. "W-what are you doing? We n-need to go."

"Put your hands behind you, before I do it.

Fred complied and Gary cuffed him. "We know about the SIM card, Fred. We know you tried to cover up the list. We know Trevor found out." Gary spun the detective around. "Where's Trevor, Fred?"

"I t-told you. We …"

"Oh, shut up." Gary looked at Tommy. "We need to find him." He heard some thrashing, and two of the unis broke into the clearing. They looked at the situation and one of them spoke.

"That's the perp? Where's the detective?"

"Missing. We have to spread out and find him." As he spoke, he heard the baying of dogs in the distance. "Canine Unit. I'll stay. You guys spread out and search. Leave the scumbag with me."

The dogs arrived and were going nuts in the center of the sumac grove. There were three teams of two dogs and three handles. They spread out and one team caught a scent, then a different team caught a second scent, leading in another direction. Gary was beginning to think maybe Fred was telling the truth when one of the handlers called out that they'd found a gun. Gary checked it out. Service issue, maybe Trevor's. He bagged it and the search continued. One of the unis took Fred back to the car. An ambulance was ordered just in case.

A cry came out from one of the handlers. Gary and Tommy rushed to the bottom of the ravine. Trevor was laying, unresponsive. No pulse or breathing. Gary started CPR.

"Screw the ambulance," he said to Tommy. "Call a medevac chopper to this location."

***

Gary was in the captain's office with Tommy and an Assistant District Attorney.

"Well, he's not talking," the ADA said. "We can't hold him. So, he bought a SIM card. Big deal."

"That is bullshit of the highest magnitude," Gary said. "He used it to phone a suspect in a murder investigation."

"We don't know that. He claims he lost the phone."

"What about kidnapping? And destroying evidence."

"His story about a tip holds water until we can question Trevor. He also claims he received the email and went for a piss. When he came back, Trevor was at his desk doing something on the computer. He says he couldn't find the email after that."

Gary threw up his hands. "That is absolute bullshit. What about the partial on Trevor's gun. There were six matching points."

"Not enough," the ADA sighed. "Look, "I can keep him in overnight, but unless he confesses, or we get a statement from that detective…"

"Harvey," Gary yelled. "His name is Detective Trevor Harvey. He's fighting for his life, and you're going to let an attempted murderer go."

The ADA squirmed. "Yes. Detective Harvey. Until we get a statement from him, Fred walks in the morning." The ADA stood. "Sorry folks. Get the statement. You've got my number."

"Okay, Sam," the captain said. "We'll be in touch." When he had left the room, Gary addressed the captain. "That's it? We just let that pencil-neck walk away."

Dan put his hands up. "Calm down detective. He's only doing his job."

"Very poorly."

"Any word on Trevor?"

Gary checked his messages. "Still being worked on. I don't know Cappy. There was a lot of blood on the ground."

"Well, I guess it's a wait out, then. Let that bastard stew in the cell for a bit and have another go at him later."

Gary cleared his throat. "There's one other thing, captain."

"Captain, eh." Dan eyed him at the use of his full title. "What'd you do now?"

"Trevor asked me to run down the GPS on the car that was outside Jenny's."

"He did, did he."

"Well, yeah. It was traced to this address. It's an out-of-the-way place. Good spot to keep to yourself if you happen to be in a questionable profession. Should we keep an eye on it?"

"I'll get a couple of guys on it." Dan was shaking his head. "Trevor asked me to … yeah, right." He flicked his hand. "Get out of here. Talk to Trevor as soon as you can."

Dan picked up the phone to arrange for surveillance.

***

The next morning Gary caught the doctor as he was making his rounds.

"Detective Johnson." The doctor shook hands. "Dr. Anderson. Let's sit over here." Once they were seated, he continued. "Mr. Harvey is quite ill. He is stable but in critical condition."

"How long before I can speak with him?"

"That is difficult to say. He is intubated and in an induced coma. If everything goes as planned, ten days to two weeks." Gary opened his mouth to speak but the doctor raised his hand. "Let me explain. He will remain in a coma for at least ten days. Then, we *may* slowly bring him out of it and assess as we go. He will still be intubated even though he is conscious, so any conversation will be difficult. This isn't TV, detective. These things take time. There is no use hanging around here. He's not coming out of it until we decide. Go home. We will call you."

Gary stood. "Thank you, doctor." They shook and Gary left the hospital. He checked with the surveillance and there was nothing to report. No activity, not even a light on last night. Something was up.

When Gary got back to the division, he found out Fred had been released, on administrative leave, with pay. He raced into the captain's office.

"What the hell, Cappy?"

"Gary, we have nothing on him. As a matter of fact, his story could have Trevor in trouble. Go out and find something new. Check those other phone numbers."

Gary left in a huff. He picked up the list of phone numbers and began chasing them down. What could he nail Fred on? There must be something. He needed to get into that house. A quick call confirmed no new activity.

He phoned the captain and got the okay for a search tomorrow morning. He collected the appropriate warrants and organized a team. He went home, satisfied everything was ready for tomorrow.

***

Gryphon finished the last of his Eggs Benedict and looked out the window of his suite at the Drake Hotel. Sailboats skimmed the waters of Lake Michigan, enjoying the light breeze. In the distance, a lake freighter carried goods to another port. *Symbolic.* He finished packing and called for the bellhop.

Ten minutes later he entered his limo which drove him to O'Hare. VIP status ensured an easy check-in. He boarded and the 11:00 o'clock plane to Atlanta left on time. The two-hour flight had him arriving at 2:00 local.

Delta stored his luggage while he took a cab to the Barclay Hotel. From there he accessed one of the business computers with a legitimate hotel card. He logged into a dating website and sent a message to a lady asking if she would be interested in going on a date. She replied she was ready, and a time was set for two days from today. An insignificant exchange, but very important in Gryphon's plans.

He ate a late lunch in the Barclay restaurant and returned to the airport, gathered his luggage, and boarded a late afternoon flight to New York. Two hours later he bordered a Lufthansa flight to Frankfurt. When the seatbelt light turned off, he checked his watch, took his cell phone out, and dialed a number. Back at his former house, the detonator activated the incendiary devices, and the house was soon in flames. He settled into his seat, sipping on his brandy.

***

It was around 7:30 that night when Gary received word of the fires from the surveillance team. He rushed over, but the fire department was still working on extinguishing the blaze. It took them close to three hours while he stood helplessly as potential evidence went up in flames.

The next morning Gary woke and drove to the house. He watched the fire marshal inspect the debris. The house was burnt to the ground, everything except the foundation destroyed.

"Can't come in yet, detective," the man called out. "I don't think you'll find much, anyways. See here." He pointed to a portion of the foundation. "That indicates a high temperature burn, maybe phosphorus. I'll have to test. If we come across anything, I'll call you."

"Yeah, thanks." He gave a wave and walked to his car.

Waiting on the doctor. Waiting on the fire marshal. Man, it was frustrating. He decided to drive to the office and track some more phone numbers.

He didn't get very far with them. After an hour or two and three numbers with dead ends, he threw his pen down and signed out of his computer. It was time to go home and take the kids out. Get his mind off work for a bit.

***

A fresh Monday morning finally brought some light to the situation. One of the phone numbers on the list from the red phone had come up in another case he had been working on with Jenny. It was associated with the human trafficking case that bastard Lefebvre was involved in. Maybe he was connected to this after all.

Gary looked up from his desk and saw an officer escorting a UPS delivery woman.

"Detective Gary Johnson?" she asked.

"Yes, that's me."

"I have a delivery for you. Can you sign here?"

Gary signed and took the package, placing it on his desk. It was about the size of a shoebox. No return address. He wondered who had sent it and what it was. *A bomb, maybe?* He looked around. There seemed to be an unusual number of people hanging around his desk. *Probably some gag from the fellows. Waiting for me to open it.* He checked with UPS online and it appeared they did scans for explosives.

Curiosity got the better of him and he tore open the outside wrapping.

***

Doctor Anderson was going over Trevor's chart. "I think we may be able to ease him out of the coma a few days early, possibly Thursday," he said to the consulting team. "His condition is improving."

They nodded.

***

It was indeed a shoebox, tapped heavily. On the lid a typewritten note said:

Detective Johnson's eyes only.

He grabbed a knife and slit the tape holding the lid. It took some effort. Man, these jokers. He had another look around. They were playing it cool, acting like they weren't looking. He flipped the lid open, waiting for some jack-in-the-box to pop out. Instead, inside was what looked like a tiny hard drive and a thick envelope. He opened it and unfolded the paper inside. It was in a large font and said:

> *Detective Johnson, or may I call you Gary? I believe I will. My name is Gryphon. I have some interesting information you may find useful. I have included recordings as proof of my statements.*

One thing I should stress before we continue. Please do not try to find me. You won't be able to. I am long gone and hidden well.

Now, on to the business at hand. I am a contract killer and was hired by an unknown person to eliminate Jenny Downey. I do not know this person's name; however, I took a picture of him when he recovered his instructions from an establishment called Cliffy's Chowdown. Subsequently, I took further pictures of him dropping off the cash. All this evidence is conveniently stored on the device I left you. I have also included voice tapings of our conversations. He really is an annoying man. That stutter drove me crazy.

Furthermore, I was also contracted by one Louis "Two Toes" Lefebvre to eliminate Jenny Downey. A kind of double payment for me. Also involved in various degrees were a "Pinky" LeChance and a Bobby Simpson. The taped conversation and a video of the transaction are included on the drive. I left a listening bug in his office and picked up some very interesting conversations about other illicit actions on behalf of Mr. Lefebvre and his associates. They include addresses and phone numbers. I hope you find them useful.

Gary, I did not eliminate your detective partner. I killed Mark Downey in self-defense. My profession may seem underhanded to you, maybe even despicable, but I am just a cog in the gear of life, like crooked politicians, greedy businessmen, or dirty cops. Besides, I may even turn over a new leaf; start fresh as you will; or not.

Either way, I hope this little package helps in any decision that may arise about pursuing me. Consider it a pre-arranged plea bargain; a get out of jail free card.

Good luck in your career, Gary. You'll be busy. There are a lot of bad people out there.

Gryphon.

Gary flopped back in his chair, wiping his face. He sat for several minutes thinking. This was incredible. If only half the things were true, this could be a game-changer. He needed to do this right.

"Tommy," he called out. "Can you come over here?"

The detective ambled over. "What's up?"

Gary gloved up. "I want you to witness what's in this package I received just now. Shoebox, envelope, letter, and this device."

"Yep, I saw it come in. What's in the note?"

Gary explained.

"Sugar shit. The motherload."

"Maybe," Gary said. "It's gotta pan out, though. Okay, thanks for witnessing this."

"No prob."

Next, Gary called forensics. While he was waiting for them to show up, he called the captain and filled him in. Then he called CIFT with a heads up of a device coming their way.

Forensics found no discernible prints, swabbed for any DNA, but were not hopeful. Gary took the device down to CIFT. One of the senior techs had a look at it.

"It's basically a small hard drive similar to one out of a laptop but capable of a higher encryption level. Let's have a look." He grabbed some cables and connected the device to a computer. "Look here. Not even encrypted. Where's the fun in that? Okay, what do we have here?" Several keystrokes later a window came up with hundreds of files in it. "There you go. A lot of pictures, some videos, and audio, too. There could be more hidden ones. I'd have to dig deeper." He looked up at Gary. "May take a while."

"Can you copy these for me?"

"Sure. Let's see. Oh, here. This one should hold them all." He grabbed another hard drive and connected it. It took a few minutes to copy the files. "There you go. Have fun."

"Thanks." Gary slapped him on the back and raced back to his desk to look at the files.

An hour later he was in the captain's office, showing him the contents.

"Holy shit," the captain said. His eyes were wide, and he was leaning back in his chair. "This is a gold mine. We've got Fred's voice on tape, pictures of him delivering the money, and this Gryphon's letter."

"We've also got Lefebvre by the short and curlies," Gary said. "Video of him hiring and paying this Gryphon, audio of human trafficking, and extortion. We've got him, Cappy."

"Well, let's move slowly. Pick up that scumbag Fred first. We'll need to verify the rest of this before we move on Lefebvre. Get Fred. I'll get the ADA."

"Will do, Cappy." Gary jumped up and headed out the door.

He called out to Tommy. "Hey, want to have some fun?"

"Sure. What's doing?"

"We're going to catch a weasel."

Tommy shrugged and followed.

***

Interrogation Room One was a three by four meter room with a table and four chairs. On one side of the table sat Fred, in handcuffs with his lawyer beside him. The ADA stared at Fred.

"Conspiracy to commit murder, kidnapping, attempted murder, illegal firing of a service weapon…"

"You can add theft, too," Gary announced, walking into the room. "He got the money from the evidence locker."

"Theft, as well. Want to talk now, Fred?"

"You can't prove any of this," Fred's lawyer spoke up.

"We'll see during the arraignment. Detective Harvey may have something to say about that." The ADA looked at Fred. "Do you have anything to say? Could help you out. Just confess and save everyone the trouble of a trial. I can arrange for a nicer facility. Cops don't do well in the general population prisons."

Fred shook his head.

"Take him away," the ADA said. "We've got him on conspiracy and theft for now."

***

Three weeks later, Trevor, out of his coma and tubing removed, gave a detailed statement sealing Fred's fate.

He was arraigned on seven charges and his trial was set for October.

***

Gary led a task force to investigate Lefebvre's activities. Although the ADA figured Gryphon's evidence may not be admissible, it was enough to get warrants. Phone lines were tapped, main characters were surveilled, financial leads were followed, and offshore accounts were checked. They'd been at it two months. It was taking a long time but the captain wanted a solid case.

Gary was finalizing the warrants and preparing the take-down as a cheer rose in the room. He looked up and saw Trevor walking in. Allie was beside him, ensuring he wasn't about to fall over. Most of his bruising was gone. He had one arm in a sling but otherwise looked well. Others were congratulating him as he made his way towards Gary.

"Hey there. How are you feeling?"

"Not bad. The collar bone is taking longer to heal than I thought, but I wanted to get back to work."

"You ready for Fred's trial? Next week, right?"

"Yeah, I'm ready. That bastard's going down. Look what he's done to me."

"That's right. Look, Trevor. I'll catch up later. I'm due in the captain's office. Welcome back."

Gary grabbed his files and entered the captain's office. They discussed the upcoming trial and moved on to the Lefebvre investigation. When they were finished, Gary hesitated at the door.

"Say Cappy. Trevor's back to work now. Neither one of us have a partner. Why don't you put the two of us together?"

"You and Trevor?"

"Yeah, why not?"

"Do you think the new Sergeant of the squad should be teamed up with a 'greenhorn' as you called him?"

"New sergeant?" Gary's jaw dropped. He put his finger to his chest. "Me?"

"Yeah, you. But keep it on the sly. I'll make an announcement later."

"Thanks, captain. What about Trev and me?"

"I thought you said he was too green. Still sucking lollipops."

"Yeah, well Kojak sucked lollipops, too.

"Get out of here." The captain waved him away, smiling.

***

Fist pumps were rampant throughout the courtroom when the jury pronounced Fred guilty on all charges. Trevor's testimony was stellar. Fred hung his head and would not make eye contact as he was led from the courtroom in cuffs.

"Time for drinks," Gary suggested.

"First round's on me," Trevor announced.

"No way," said the captain. "You're not paying for any rounds. Okay, everyone. Off to Casey's."

They settled into the bar, everyone having a good time toasting Trevor and anyone else that came to mind.

All Gary could think of was the last time he was here with Jenny, a week before she died.

***

Nestled amongst the foothills of the Alps in southern Germany is the town of Fussen. It is mostly famous for the nearby Neuschwanstein Castle but otherwise unremarkable unless you considered the views. Bordering

Austria, it was surrounded by forests and lakes. One lake, the Forggensee, was the habitat for several townhouse chalets and single homes. One such home was occupied by a single man who had been here for about six months now.

Gryphon sat on his balcony overlooking the lake, a brandy by his side. He enjoyed his new life tucked away here out of sight. Munich was less than an hour away to the east, Switzerland to the west.

After Frankfurt, he had flown to London, switched from Heathrow to Gatwick, then on to Paris, and finally, Munich. He met with an acquaintance who provided the keys to this house and a new Mercedes. After six months he was familiar with the area and felt comfortable.

Next week he was heading to the Black Forest for some cross-country skiing. He preferred it to downhill and the Schonach region was one of the best. Two weeks on the trails, staying at a spa chalet with a pool and sauna. He was waiting for the confirmation. Gryphon took another sip of brandy as his cell phone rang.

It was not his red phone. He did not have a red one anymore.

***

"Foreman of the jury, have you reached a decision?"

"Yes, we have, your honor."

"What say you?"

"On the twenty-three counts of human trafficking, we find the defendant, Louis Lefebvre, *guilty*."

"On the charges of kidnapping, we find the defendant *guilty*."

"On the charges of forcible confinement, we find the defendant *guilty*."

"On the charge of conspiracy to commit murder, we find the defendant *guilty*."

The jury forewoman continued as the front row of detectives breathed a sigh of relief. When the jury was finished the judge excused them and "Two Toes" was led from the courtroom.

Captain Dan Ridley, sitting in the front row, looked at the rest of them.

"Great job guys. I guess we're heading to Casey's again. Been a lot of this since our new sergeant took over." He slapped Gary on the back. "First rounds on you, Sarge."

Half an hour later they were ordering their second round.

"So," Gary asked. "I guess the ADA is not trying to follow this Gryphon fellow?"

"Nope," Dan answered. "Gryphon admitted he was a hitman, but never confessed to any hits except Jenny's, which he didn't do. We have no outstanding homicides that fit a hit. Plus, as he suggested, we got a lot of evidence from him. He's gone and we'll leave it at that."

"Wonder where he is?"

"If I were him," Dan thought out loud. "I'd be hunkered down in the Caribbean somewhere." He nodded at Gary's drink. "Want another?"

"Nah, I got something I need to do."

A light January breeze blew the fluffy snowflakes about, not letting them land on the grassy landscape of the cemetery. Gary pulled his coat collar up against the chill. Her gravestone was just ahead. He carried a bouquet of artificial flowers and placed them in the holder. Kneeling, he touched the stone. She was good people, one of the better detectives he'd worked with.

"We got them, kiddo. Both of them. You can rest easy, now."

The wind swirled and rustled the flowers. He thought he heard a voice whispering "Thank you."

A WESTERN STORY

This was done as a fun exercise with my writing group.

Dirk Bennet shifted in his saddle, astride his chestnut mare, overlooking the nameless village which centered in the valley along the Animas River. The river bent around to his left in a gentle arc, then worked its way back a mile further down to form a perfect "C", a nice little niche for this sleepy hamlet.

Might be a spot to settle in, I reckon.

Dirk fished out his prayer book and rolled a cigarette, struck a match on his chaps, and lit the end. He drew in, held it, savoring the moment, and slowly released through his nose. The smoke curled around, drifting toward his horse. She shook her head and snorted, working the bit.

"Whoa, Olive. Settle down now. Let me enjoy this one." She stomped and flicked her tail in protest. Dirk smiled. Best horse he ever had, but wouldn't let him have a smoke. He drew in a few more as he contemplated his next move. He was two days south of Durango, Colorado and into New Mexico territory. Two weeks on the road now. This looked like a quiet little town. Off the main trails, with only this dusty trail leading south. The main route was to the west through La

Plata. Could he make a go of it here? Enough farms that he could pick up some work. The question was, was he far enough away? He took one last drag, pinched the end off, and urged Olive down the trail. He passed a weathered sign saying Cedar Gulch, Pop 89. The nine had been recently painted over what looked like a seven.

Good, they're accepting newcomers.

He pondered the name, as there were no cedars in sight. It didn't really matter; it was just a name. About two dozen buildings spread evenly on either side of one street, which positioned itself north-south. All one floor except two, more likely the saloon and the stables. Several farms circled the town, all within the gentle C of the river. He rode down the street, a tumbleweed bounding by as he passed a general store and a few houses, stopping at the saloon.

Dirk tied Olive to the hitchin' post outside Molly's Saloon and removed his black Stetson. He dipped his hand in the cool water of the trough, scrubbed his face, then ran his hands through his hair several times, and replaced his hat. "Be back in a bit, ole girl. Need to wet the whistle." She whinnied her approval and slurped some water.

Dirk pushed through the batwing doors. Very little sunlight passed through the grimy windows, making the interior dark and dingy. Several empty tables dotted the dusty hardwood floor. One, off to the left, had four men at it playing cards. A bar took up the better half of the back wall on the left, behind it stood a man and a healthy supply of bottles. To the bar's right, a set of stairs led up to the second floor, where a banister went across the whole length of the upstairs. Dirk could visualize the ladies leaning on it at night, waiting for business. A hallway led to the rooms on the upper floor towards the back. An old piano off to the right completed the lower level. He tipped his hat to the men and strolled up to the bar. "I'll have a whiskey and a bite to eat." He settled on to the stool as the balding bartender poured him a shot.

"Welcome stranger. I'll get some vittles out momentarily. You just passin' through?"

"That depends. Might want to settle in here if there's any work to be had."

"Hmmm... mostly farm work is all. The Jenkins may need a seasonal guy, four months at best, then there's the Henrys, same thing. Ole Dan might need occasional help at the stables. He fancies himself a farrier and blacksmith. Hit and miss. 'scuse me, be right back with your vittles." Dirk watched the man head through a doorway and a few minutes later return with some stew and a piece of bread. "So where do you hail from?"

"North of here. You wouldn't know the place so there's not much use naming it." Dirk removed his hat, placed it on the stool beside him and ran his fingers through his hair again, before digging into the stew.

"Fine by me. You have a name?" Dirk was about to give him a name when one of the men at the table behind him spoke out.

"He's got a name all right." Dirk heard the scrapping of chair legs. He spun around on his stool and saw a man standing at the table with the card players. That's when he saw the star pinned on the left of the man's shirt. "That dirty, rotten, thieving, murdering scoundrel is known as The Colorado Kid."

***

Ben Stillman, sheriff of Cedar Gulch, sat with three of his friends, playing poker when a stranger ambled into Molly's Saloon, tipped his hat, and went to the bar. He had his back to the wall, always did, it was better that way as a lawman, and studied the tall man. Something about him didn't feel right. He couldn't put a finger on it, just a tingle in his neck, something that after 15 years as sheriff he'd learned to listen too.

"You playin' or daydreamin'?" It was Clyde Fessterman, the town doctor, apothecary, and vet, nudging his arm. "How many?"

"Three." Ben kept his eye on the stranger while the doc dealt him three cards. What was it about him? He took a quick look at his cards and threw them down. "I'm out."

"You're always out. That wife of yourn got you on a limit?" It was Hank Middleton, a cattle farmer. It was another three weeks before he would be busy driving his cattle to Santa Fe. For now, he enjoyed the afternoon poker games.

"No limit on me, old-timer. Just know how to play the game." Ben replied. He kept staring at the stranger. "I'm out the next hand."

"What's itchin' your craw?"

"Nothin', just play."

Ben listened to Jimmy Dooright, the bartender, and strangely enough, owner of Molly's Saloon, talking up the stranger. The guy was asking about work around here. That was a laugh. Not much going in this town. It was so far away from anything most folks forgot it existed. Ben often had to ride into Farmington to remind that old clerk at the regional office to pay him. He'd just done that, nigh on three days ago.

Jimmy came back with the stranger's food and asked where he hailed from. Up north, eh. That's odd, can't name yer home town. Then it hit Ben. He'd seen the stranger's picture in the window of the Farmington sheriff's office. Wanted for thirteen counts of murder, twelve bank robberies, and burning down a town. Well dust me off and call me hornswoggled. No chance by cracker. He stood up, forcing his chair back and called out.

***

Dirk eyed the man, obviously the sheriff in this shit-hole town, sizing him up. His gun wasn't drawn, a big mistake on his behalf, as far as Dirk was concerned, and he looked a little hesitant. Too long in this town without any adversity, no real lawbreakers to deal with, going through the motions.

Looky here, sheriff," he tendered the first offering. "I don't want any trouble and neither do you, but if you go fer that there gun of yourn, all three of your poker buddies will be dead before you know it." His eyes flickered as he held up his left hand, finger extended. His right hand remained by his holster. "Nah, ah, ah, mister bartender. Don't you be reachin' down for that rifle, ya hear. Move around front real slow, like, where I can see ya. Hands up." He heard Jimmy shuffling from behind the bar, saw him out front with his hands high in the air, then addresses the sheriff. "We don't need a big shoot-up here, with a bunch of people dead, although I'm quite happy to oblige. You just let me ride on out of here and everyone can go back to their lives."

"Please Ben," it was the bartender. "I don't want no dust-up in here. Just let things be. Let him go."

"Shut up, Jimmy. I'll handle this. I'm takin' you in, mister.

"Listen to Jimmy, Ben. I'd just as likely shoot yous all, as spit in this here 'toon right here." His left hand motioned to the metal bucket by his stool, then moved back to the second holster. "Now, I wants yous all to get down on the floor real slow like. No sudden movements 'cause I got a awful twitchy trigger finger."

"Not happenin', mister." It was the sheriff.

"Well then. It looks like we got ourselves one of them there, what's ya call it, a Mexican Standoff. Well, I'm gonna put up with it fer about ten seconds and then it'll be all over."

"Leave these men out of it." the sheriff spoke. "You and I can take this outside."

"Ooheeee. A shoot-out in Cedar Gulch!" Dirk smiled. "I'll oblige ya, sheriff, but these here others are still gonna' kiss planks, whilen we get ourselves set up, now."

The two men stared each other down. Dirk felt indifference to the situation. He'd been shooting men down for a long time now and this was no different.

"You," he motioned to the bartender, "Over with the others and start smoochin' with the floor." He watched Jimmy scurry to the table and drop. He nodded to the others. "You too. Real slow, like." They looked at each other.

"Do what he says, boys." It was the sheriff. "And stay in here. I'll look after him."

"I'm gonna back on outta here and get myself set up. No need not worry, old man. I may be a killer and a thief, but I'm not without honor. I'll shoot you fair and square." Dirk backed out of the saloon, keeping his eye on the sheriff, and glancing around for any other trouble. This deadbeat duster wouldn't last long. He'd shoot him and high tail it outta here.

Both men positioned themselves in the center of the street, about fifty feet apart. The sun shone from the west, to the right of Dirk's shoulder, the sheriff's left, neither with an advantage. They stood for close to thirty seconds staring each other down, waiting for the other to flinch. Dirk caught a slight movement and drew. He watched as the sheriff matched him for speed, but his shot went first, the lawman just after. The sheriff spun to his left, clutching his chest as a searing pain raged through Dirk's stomach. The sheriff dropped to the ground face first, motionless as Dirk checked his stomach. Blood poured out his right side. He checked and it was not through, so he removed his bandana around his neck and held it against the hole. A stab of pain shot through his body. He'd have to dig that slug out later, but it was time to beat it on out of here. He staggered over to Olive and struggled up into the saddle, turned to the south and rode off.

On the outskirts of town, he came across another population sign. He took the time to use his blood-soaked bandana to change the nine to an eight. He thought it appropriate the loss of the town's sheriff should be marked in blood. The trail led to a river crossing where he forded it without problems and made his way to the ridge on the south bank. One last look at Cedar Gulch, there was no posse chasing him, and he turned his horse to the south. With a defiant flick of her tail, she trotted off.

It would be two more hours before he lost consciousness from blood loss and slipped out of his saddle.

***

Meanwhile, back in Cedar Gulch, Jimmy, Hank, and the doc ran out to the prone body in the middle of the street.

"Lands sake, that thar bastard done shot him."

"That's what happens durin' a shoot out, Jimmy." It was Clyde, the doctor. Here help me turn him over. I see no blood. It wasn't a through shot."

"Oh, lord, I can't stand the sight of blood."

"Well go fetch my bag then. Hank and me'll look after it." Clyde shook his head as the bartender tore off up the street. A couple of townsfolk drifted from their homes, curious, but keeping their distance. He checked for a pulse. It was weak and rapid. "He's still alive. Ok, Hank, we're gonna turn him over real slow, like. You grab his legs and I'll take his shoulders. Easy now. Yep. Just like that. Hang on. Gotta steady his head."

A huge hole was torn on the left breast of the sheriff's shirt and blood spread around it. Clyde bent over listening for his breath. It was rapid and shallow. He began to unbutton the shirt looking around. "Where's that stupid bartender?"

Jimmy came running up. Here's your bag, doc... oh man, look at that blood. He's dead, ain't he?" He leaned over and threw up.

"Good grief, Jimmy, take that shit elsewhere." Clyde grabbed his scissors and cut the sheriff's shirt. A hole, near two inches wide dominated the left chest area. The doc poured some whiskey on it to wash the blood away. A scream came from the sheriff's mouth, and they all jumped back.

"That hurts like hell." Ben's eyes focused on the doc. "You crazy sawbones. What happened?"

"You got shot, Ben. Looks bad. Hold yer horses, here. Hank, hand me those leathers and that clamp, will ya. No, no. The other one. Ya, that's it. Now Ben, take a few swallers of this whiskey. Jimmy, go fetch another bottle. Ben, clamp down on this here leather. I'm gonna pour some more juice on that wound."

"What's going on here?" It was Dan, making his way over from the stables.

"Sheriff done got himself shot," Hank answered. "Some gunslinger called the Colarader Kid."

"Looking mighty bad, I reckon. Shall I start on the pine box?"

"Shut up you idiot." Doc glared at him. "He can still hear ya."

"Here's that whiskey." Jimmy had returned. "It's the rot gut. Should work well."

Clyde poured the fluid on the wound and Ben screamed through gritted teeth. "Well lookee here, would you." The doc dug into the sheriff's chest with the forceps as the prone man growled and kicked his feet. Dust billowed up around the temporary operating theater. "Now stop that fussing, Ben. It don't help none. Oh, here we are." He gave one final tug and the forceps popped out of Ben's chest. Clamped on the end was a mangled sheriff's badge and dead center of the star was the bullet from The Colorado Kid that should have killed him. "That there gall darn bullet hit your badge, Ben." The sheriff was thrashing around too much to nod any acknowledgment. "Pushed that there star in some but no real damage. Might have a cracked rib, and your nipple is all buggered to hell, but you're likely not be needing it, I reckon."

Dan slapped his thigh. "I told you that badge was better than a tin one. I done did saved his life, I reckon."

"Polly-hocs! You just never had any tin to make one. Had to use steel. Ben, here had to shine it up near every day, causa your mistake. However, I reckon you done saved his life as a result." Clyde looked at the others. "Hold him down steady like, whiles I stitch him. Ben this is going to hurt some so take another swig and bite down on those leathers."

After Ben was stitched up and the bleeding stopped, they moved him to his house, and he rested in bed with an ample supply of whiskey.

***

It was ten days after the shooting and Ben and Jimmy were taking Jimmy's buggy to Farmington. Ben wanted to report the sighting of the Colorado Kid and Jimmy needed supplies. They headed south, crossed the river, and worked their way along the path. Around three hours into their trip, they spotted a horse in the distance near a creek. Above it, some buzzards were circling. As they came closer Ben noticed something dangling from a stirrup. One of the buzzards swooped down, but the horse charged it, chasing it into flight. Ben saw it was a cowpoke stuck in the stirrup. Jimmy stopped the buggy and Ben eased down, wincing as his chest muscles flexed.

"By gore Jimmy." Ben looked up. "If'n it ain't that Colarader Kid. Come-on. Help me fetch him onto the wagon."

Jimmy helped wrestle the outlaw into the back and tied the horse up. They continued to the town. "Cracker Joe, Ben. Never thought we'd come across the likes of that one. No siree."

***

Ben walked away from the sheriff's office in Farmington. He had the reward money stuffed in his pockets and he made his way to the general store. He ordered up a new forge for Dan and even got him some tin along with the rest of the metals he needed. Figured he owed him that much.

AN UNUSUAL FAIRY TALE

Things were going to change for Vince now. Probably for the worse. Three weeks in solitary would seem bad enough but returning to gen-pop could only mean more trouble. Trouble for him and trouble for his cellmate. Vince thought back three weeks ago when he tore his former cellmate's head almost completely off. It happened during one of his "confused" times. The times when he just blacked out and did crazy things.

Now they were placing him back in a regular cell. He hoped it was a single one. Taggert, one of the guards, walked beside him. He was a prick, one of the worst ones. He catered to the skinheads and hated Vince.

The door slid open as two female guards glared at him. Taggert shoved him through, and they made their way down the corridors. They traversed through several doors and multiple hallways until Taggert stopped him in front of a cell at the end of a row. There was only one bed in there. No cellmate to lose his head. Vince said a silent prayer, to whom he did not know, but thought it couldn't hurt. He stepped in the cell and offered his hands for the removal of the cuffs. As Taggert twisted the last cuff, he leaned in and whispered.

"I'll be back tonight."

Vince's knees buckled slightly as the blood rushed from his head, making him woozy. No cellmate, but the bastard would be back.

No rest for the wicked.

***

Supper came and went. A guard brought his personal effects, items he wasn't allowed in solitary. He spent some time arranging them, thinking about what had landed him in jail. The two women. A month apart. Both were brutally murdered. Betty Hardy, a single mother, with a seven-year-old boy. He had torn off her arm. The boy was living with an aunt. Deborah Henning, mother of two and loving wife. She had her chest sliced open, and organs removed. He hadn't really done it, or so he thought. It was during his "confused" times. He shouldn't be here in jail. He should be in a hospital being treated.

He knew he had problems. It had started about a year ago, shortly after he'd returned from that animal study in Alberta. He worked as a field research Zoologist at Guelph University and made many field trips. At first, he had just blacked out, losing a few hours until he woke again. Then, each blackout got worse. One time his apartment looked like it was ransacked, tables knocked over, curtains torn, curious scratch marks on the furniture. His "confused" time usually came during times of stress.

Things got progressively worse. Like when he ravaged those two women. That's what put him in jail in the first place. Then, not even a month into time served, he attacked his cellmate.

Ten o'clock came and the lights went out. He waited nervously for Taggert to come. It would be another couple of hours. The guard needed to wait until the rest were asleep.

Midnight passed. He heard footsteps approaching and they stopped at his cell. It was Taggert. The guard motioned for him to place his hands in the opening. He was cuffed and he backed off to the far end of the cell, anticipating a beatdown. Taggert unlocked the door and motioned him forward. Vince hesitated. This was unusual.

"Let's go." The guard whispered. "We're going to the laundry room."

Vince had worked here a couple of times before solitary and remembered it as a loud, bustling place. He stepped out from his cell and just like earlier today they walked down the dark hallway. They arrived at the laundry door, and he waited as the guard unlocked it. Vince imagined several skinheads inside, ready to beat him. Sweat formed on his forehead. He was already getting a tingling in his spine. They stepped inside to a darkened room. Taggert flicked the light switch. A half-dozen inmates were standing in a semicircle.

"This is for Sammy," Taggert whispered in his ear.

Taggert was going to enjoy this. Nothing better than a good pounding. He turned and locked the door, then placed his back to it to watch the show. The six inmates were still standing, staring in disbelief. Taggert looked at Vince. The inmate's nose bulged, and his face protruded and elongated toward him. Glowing, red eyes stared at Taggert. Its ears grew longer and flattened backward against its neck. His hair grew at an alarming rate. A deep guttural sound emanated from the long saliva-dripping mouth. *Like a dog.* But the dog was standing upright, on powerful hind legs. Long dangly arms ended in huge hands and sharp claws. The Vince-creature snapped the handcuffs like string. It was that which sprung the inmates into action.

They circled the snarling creature, clubs swinging. It was hard to attack with it snapping and swinging its arms. One inmate got too close, and his midsection tore open from the long claws. The creature leapt on another, biting their head. The rest moved in but hesitated when the creature swirled around eyeing its prey. This was no longer a beatdown. It was survival. Taggert fumbled with his keys and dropped them as the beast approached him. The others took the opportunity to attack. One managed to bring his club down on the creature's left arm. Bones snapped as the Vince-creature roared. Taggert felt a brief hope but it subsided as the creature swung its good arm around and clawed another inmate, biting at another. The creature swiped at Taggert, and an explosion of pain was the last he knew of this world.

***

It was close to six in the morning when Vince woke up. A few streetlamps cast enough light through the large windows for him to see. The sky was heavily overcast and raining. His left arm throbbed, and he was unsure where he was. He had a funny taste in his mouth and there was a foul smell in the air. A familiar smell. He sat up, cradling his arm. He ached all over; every joint was on fire. There was blood all over him. Several crumpled bodies lay around him. It was all coming back to him. Taggert. The inmates. He struggled off the table, grimacing with each jolt of pain. One inmate's stomach was opened, and organs dangled from the table. Another's head was crushed and mauled beyond recognition. His "confused" times. But Vince knew. It looked just like those women. An arm lay on the floor several feet away. One eye kept an accusing stare on Vince.

Several industrial washers and driers lined one wall. The centre area consisted of numerous tables for folding sheets. The outer wall was mainly large windows, with louvered openings occupying the upper third, normally opened to let the heat escape. He could see some of Lincoln Street and, in the distance, lights from the "mountain". Clouds rolled by and the trees swayed from a swift breeze. The lighter sky was promise of morning.

He had to get out of here. The cellmate had been bad enough, but this would be his end. The rest of the guards would make sure he was dead by the end of the day. Roll call would be soon. He searched through Taggert's pockets then spotted the ring of keys on the floor. He glanced at the door leading to the outside. Then he looked down at himself. His clothes were a mess, blood-soaked and torn. So were Taggert's and the others. He scrambled over to the lockers. Sometimes the guards had their uniforms done here instead of at home. He searched through several lockers, but no such luck. There were only the bright orange prison jumpsuits, worm by inmates when outside the prison, not the best when trying to escape a city. He decided to stick with his tattered clothes and found a sink to wash in. Next, he needed to immobilize his arm and searched high and low for a splint. He could find nothing, then decided to use Taggert's baton. He stripped a bedsheet down and managed to tie it off. Man, he could use some ibuprofen right now. One last look at the mess, and he went to the door leading outside.

He was trying all the different keys when he realized the door may be alarmed. He pondered this dilemma but figured he could do nothing about it, so he continued his quest for the correct key. Half-way through the thirty keys or so, he found success and twisted the lock. He paused for a moment and pushed the door open, racing out into the pouring rain. There was no sound of an alarm. He closed the door and surveyed the area. To his left were a couple of cube trucks backed up to delivery doors. The parking lot was around the other side, but he didn't want to hang around here too long. He needed to move into the heart of the city and lose himself; maybe heist a car somehow. A small street was close by, and he hurried south along it as nonchalantly as possible.

When Vince opened the door to the outside of the laundry room, a sensor sent an electrical charge to a relay above the door. This relay was supposed to activate the alarm and send a signal to the monitoring room where the guards would have seen which door had been breached. Unfortunately, the relay was an older, mechanical one, with movable parts. Years of humidity in the laundry room had rusted the contacts and they failed to connect, and the breach went unnoticed.

Vince zig-zagged through the streets, as the rain poured down, until he came to a back alley. There were too many people walking the streets and lots of cars. Everyone was going to work. He slinked along the alley until he came to a dumpster. It was as good a place as any. The lid squealed as he lifted it, but at least the rain and thunder masked the noise. He managed to squirm his way in without jarring his arm.

He waited for some time before he dared venture from the metal bin. The alley was quiet, and he hoped it would stay that way with everyone hunkered down at their desks. He darted from hiding spot to hiding spot until he came to a small parking lot. He was drenched, and smelt like a pig, but the rain was letting up. At least some of the blood was washing away. Four cars were parked there. None of them had their keys in the ignition. He checked under the wheel wells and bumpers and was rewarded when he found a magnetic key holder. It took several attempts to get the thing to slide open using one hand. There was a key in it, and he looked around before pressing the fob. The car's lights blinked, and he heard the click of the locks. His heart raced while he stared at each of the nearby doors leading to various buildings. He eased the car door open. With great care, he managed to get seated. Then he reached across his body with his good arm, struggling to grasp the door handle. Finally, he closed the door with a soft click. Not enough. He opened the door and slammed it a little harder to drive it home. The interior light stayed on for a maddening amount of time. He was completely exposed while waiting for the stupid light. Eventually, it began to fade, and the headlights shut off. He was about to relax when one of the doors flew open and someone stepped out.

Vince jumped and banged his bad arm on the steering wheel. He bit his knuckles waiting for the pain to subside. Eyeing outside, he wiggled down in his seat. The person surveyed the parking lot, one hand still holding the release bar. He eased the door shut, then pulled out a cell phone. Vince could swear he saw him punch in only three numbers before bringing the phone up to his ear. Beads of sweat collected into droplets and flowed down his forehead. A soft, familiar tingle began in his spine. *Breathe. Breathe. Relax.* He squirmed further down in his seat. Cellphone-man talked for what seemed like an eternity before placing the phone in his pocket. He walked to a car two over from Vince and got in, started it, and drove away. The tingle subsided.

Vince sat frozen, unable to move. He knew he needed to get out of there, but he could not trigger his muscles to respond. The distant wail of a siren bumped him out of it, and he started the car, pulling out down an alley away from the sound. Whether the siren was for him or not, he didn't care. He dodged trash cans while the ding, ding, ding of the seatbelt warning got louder. Eventually, he made it to a main street and, when he figured he was far enough away, pulled into a McDonald's parking lot at the junction of King and Main.

He needed a plan. Well, he needed clothes and heavy-duty painkillers, among other things. Most of all he needed a place to hold up for a while. Out of curiosity, he tapped the vehicle's nav system. It was amazing what you could find out about a person from their location's list. A home address in Westdale, several marked Dairy Queens, a couple of synagogues, a university in Toronto, and, oh, what was this? An address near Kearney, up by Huntsville. Beaver Lake Lane to be exact. He zoomed in with the map. It looked to be out in the boonies, probably a cottage. Nobody would be up there this late in October. Maybe a good place to recuperate. There might even be some clothes up there, and a first aid kit. It was three hundred and twelve kilometres there and he had four hundred and ninety-three in the tank. He set it as the destination and pulled out onto Main Street.

***

Laura Goldstein cut up the last of the potatoes and brought them over to Kevin. She was volunteering in a soup kitchen preparing lunch. She did this as often as she could, usually Saturdays. She had arrived at 4:00 AM. Kevin was the cook, and he was overseeing the meats. The rest of the volunteers were out front preparing the steam trays. The doors would open in fifteen minutes and hundreds of needy would file through.

Laura walked over to a hotplate where a pot of soup was simmering. She stirred the ingredients and drew in a deep breath of the savory aroma. *Chicken Penicillin.* This was her side project for this morning. Her grandmother was not feeling well, and she was bringing this soup to help her feel better. She had some lung issues and had left the city to spend some time in fresher air. The family owned a cottage up north so she had asked Laura to take her there for a week or two. Laura argued, but to no avail, and reluctantly drove her. She worried about her grandmother because most of the cottages up there were empty, their owners having winterized them and retreated to the city. Her grandmother was alone, without transportation. *Don't worry. I'll be fine. Besides Helen and Tommy are often up here.* Helen, their nearest neighbour, and her twelve-year-old son, Tommy, often went up this time of year. And her grandmother had a cell phone, although reception was dodgy. Laura relaxed. After the first wave was fed, she was heading north to visit for the weekend. Her grandmother would love the soup.

An hour later she was drying the last of the cooking pots. She packed them away and walked out to the front. Things were beginning to slow down, and she air-kissed the other volunteers, said her goodbyes, and grabbed the handle of the large thermos filled with soup. She waved goodbye to Kevin and opened the back door into the parking lot.

She pressed her fob to unlock the door to her car as she stepped into the small parking lot. She stopped when she realized something was not right, although she couldn't think what it was. Then it came to her. The click. She didn't hear the click. She pressed the fob again, her eyes scanning the small parking lot, and now she noticed her car was missing. Shaking her head, she turned back to the door, smiling. *Must have parked out front.* It was not like her to forget something like that. She was worrying about her grandmother too much nowadays.

"Hey Laura," Kevin said. "Forget something?"

"I parked out front, I guess."

"No, you didn't. I parked beside you when I got here. You're out back."

"Well, the car's not back there."

"What?" Kevin wiped his hands and motioned to the back door. "Let's see."

Laura shrugged her shoulders and followed. Kevin opened the door and stopped.

"It was right there," he pointed. "In that open spot beside my car. That's weird."

Laura began to worry. "I'll check out front." Two minutes later she was on the street and could not see her car. Just to be sure she wandered around the block and entered the back alley again, hoping to spot it, but it was not around. Time to call the cops.

***

Maddie Goldstein shifted in her chair and put down her book. The sun shone in through the window and warmed her bones. She liked the cottage and was glad she convinced her granddaughter to bring her up here. Poor Laura, always fretting so. Nothing could go wrong up here. The furnace was two years old, she had plenty of food, and Helen and Tommy were probably up for the week.

Through the living room window was a nice view overlooking the lake. A couple of trees were in the way, but she could still see well enough. It was funny, trees got older and stronger, people got older and frailer. She coughed a few times and spit out some phlegm into a tissue. She took a sip of ginger ale. Last night the full moon had been wonderful, reflecting off the water. Tonight, was supposed to be clear as well. Laura and her could watch it together. She was coming up for the weekend and would probably bring some soup. She usually arrived by five which was still three hours away. Maddie was an early riser because she loved to watch the lake, the loons, and any wildlife that walked along the shore. Often, she saw deer drinking by the lakeside.

With a couple of attempts, she pushed herself out of the chair and shuffled towards the kitchen. One of the floorboards creaked and she thought it sounded a bit like her old bones. She'd have to have that looked at. *Don't want to be falling through, now.* In the kitchen she eyed the cupboards and cleared her head. Time to bake some cookies. They would go well with the soup. Tommy would wander over soon, and he could taste test them. He somehow managed to show up just as they were coming out of the oven. That boy had a great nose. He always cleaned up for her and did all the dishes, after making sure she didn't want to make one more batch. What a scamp.

But first it was time for a piece of chocolate cake. She withdrew it from the fridge and placed it on the counter. Boy, it looked yummy. Just a little piece though; she'd be sampling the cookies later. Her cake knife sat in the knife block on top of the counter. It was old, some fifty years now, a gift for her wedding. She had cut her wedding cake with it and many more since then. Pure silver and beautifully decorated. Tommy liked looking at the ornate designs and always asked if he could cut his own piece of cake. She usually let him, but with supervision, of course. She munched on her slice as she reminisced of times with her husband.

After some time, she collected all her ingredients and spread them over the ample counter space. Laura had added an island to the kitchen, creating extra room. She busied herself mixing ingredients as she hummed a song from the old country. There was no recipe book in sight.

***

Tommy Anderson woke sharply at 7:00 AM. He needed no alarm clock but jumped out of bed and quietly got dressed. Mom would be asleep for another couple of hours, and he didn't want to wake her. He snuck into the kitchen and made a peanut butter and Nutella sandwich. This was his morning staple, and always with three pieces of bread. Peanut butter on the two outside pieces, and Nutella on both sides of the inner slice. He chewed on that and washed it down with orange juice.

Today was a busy day. He planned some exploring and rock climbing, maybe some pirating or dragon slaying. The old gravel pit needed checking on. He always found pretty rocks there, some even worth something. Then there was always Mrs. Goldstein's cookies to think about. It was Saturday and Laura would be up with some soup for her grandmother. He loved both the cookies and soup.

He made a second sandwich, this time only two slices and just peanut butter, stuffed it in his pocket, and put everything away. He snuck out the back door and bounded into the woods. It took close to an hour to walk the kilometer to the gravel pit, fighting off dragons, saving fair maidens, and playing Tarzan. Lots of his friends played robots and transformers but those weren't real.

The gravel pit was no more than a communal area to pick up fill for all the makeshift lanes leading to cottages. It comprised of all sorts of rocks and debris. Tommy found his first shiny stone here two years ago and made regular visits, rooting through the different types of rocks. He often spent hours here.

After one small quartz piece and a chunk of feldspar, he decided to call it quits. It was close to lunchtime, so he sat and ate his sandwich. With his treasures safely stowed in his pocket, he grabbed his sword/stick and ventured into the enchanted forest on the other side of the pit to duke it out with a bunch of ogres. He was careful not to go in too far, especially down this one trail. It was rumoured a young couple got lost in here a few years back.

He slashed and hacked all the ogres until he finally met the boss. It was an epic battle, but with a final thrust, he gutted the vile beast, ending evil throughout the land and saving mankind. He wrapped his wounds in magic leaves before heading back towards Mrs. Goldstein's. It was 3:00 already. Time for some cookies. First, though, he needed to stash his rocks in his tree fort.

A half hour later he came to the tree. It was conveniently spaced equal distance between his cottage and the Goldstein's. From thirty feet up, he had a good sightline on both buildings, especially now that most of the leaves had fallen. Tommy scampered up and seated himself on the four-by-four platform, made from a wooden pallet someone had dumped at the gravel pit. It had taken him two days to drag it here. Then it had taken another three days to hoist the pallet up here using some rope from a neighbour. It was fastened by wire and a few nails.

He had quite a stash of precious items stored here. Besides his pretty rocks, there was a ton of comic books, a hunting knife he had found in the woods, a brooch from Jenny McAllister, a pipe from his late father with some tobacco, binoculars, a makeshift bow, and a picture magazine that would have gotten him in a lot of trouble with his mom. He spent lots of time there, whittling sticks and pretending to smoke the pipe. One time he tried to smoke it for real but felt sick. Most of his stuff was stored in a metal container he had found under the Goldstein's cottage.

There was a crawlspace at the cottage, surrounded by lattice and chicken wire. One day, when no one was around, he found a broken piece of lattice and crawled in to see what might be under there. That was where he found the metal container, so he "borrowed" it for his treasures. There was lots of old stuff under there, but the coolest was a secret trap door that led to a magical kingdom only knights could enter. It swung upwards into the Goldstein's laundry/mudroom at the back. As much as Tommy wanted to, he dared not enter their cottage without Maddie or Laura there. His mom would give him a whooping.

***

Vince was making great time, but the pain was becoming excruciating. He needed painkillers but had no money. There was meter change in the console, but it amounted to just over two bucks. He figured he may have to rob a store or ransack a house. The house was a better option; they were spread out up here in the country. He was approaching Washago according to a sign he'd just passed, service roads on either side of the highway lined with homes spread far enough apart. They were not farmhouses, nor were they large homes of the affluent. Older homes, most with at least one rusty car sunk in the weeds in the back yard, white clapboards, and triangle TV antenna towers with no heads.

Vince pulled off Highway 11 and mentally tossed a coin. He'd try the western service road first. He crossed over the highway and headed south along the small road. Several of the houses had cars in the driveway. It was Saturday and he began to wonder if anyone was at work. He traveled past a dozen houses before he saw a car backing out a driveway two houses up. He drove by. It was an older couple with a toddler in a car seat. Great. Off to town for some shopping or something. Grandparents and the grandkid. They won't mind if I borrow some clothes and drugs. He drove a little, then doubled back and entered their driveway.

The back door offered a convenient glass window which he broke with one of the many rocks lying around. He reached in and felt the latch, twisting it. He entered the kitchen and had a good listen. Nothing. The cupboards revealed little of interest, and he moved on to the rest of the house. In the downstairs medicine cabinet was a bottle of extra strength, arthritic Tylenol. He fought with the lid using his good hand and finally got it opened. After popping two he pocketed the bottle and climbed the stairs to the bedrooms.

Grandpa had poor fashion sense as all he could find were coveralls and red or blue plaid shirts. He opted out on the formally white, now grey, underwear and went regimental. An Elmer Fudd hat completed his ensemble. His prison crocks would have to do because his feet were too big for grandpa's shoes. He fought with wool socks until he finally slid them on. His prison clothes went in a garbage bag.

Next came a supply of food. Two loaves of bread, apples and oranges, cookies, and several slices of leftover roast beef. He grabbed the food and old clothes and placed them in the car. Ten minutes later he was heading north on Highway 11 again. An hour and a half left to drive.

***

At first, the police wanted Laura to come down to the main station and make a report. Then, with word of the jailbreak, someone put two and two together and a team was dispatched. Sgt. James recorded her information as two others scoured the alley for any evidence.

"So, at no time did you go out back after you parked the car?"

"No. I came around four. Kevin was here around quarter to five." She motioned to the cook. "Everyone else comes in the front door, usually by seven. Doors open at seven-thirty, and we serve breakfast. Then we start preparing lunch. It's served at one and starts winding down by two-thirty. I went out the back and my car was gone."

"Okay, Maam. Was there anything of value visible inside the car?"

"Please. Call me Laura. No. My purse and phone were in here. Nothing in the car."

The back door opened, and a young officer approached. "No glass on the ground or any scrapings or paint. It was clean. The guy was good. We found some footprints in the mud down the alley. Looks like crocks." He looked from Laura to the Sergeant. "Maybe from the jail."

Sgt. James nodded. "Thanks, Jimmy. You can wrap it up. Thanks." He turned to Laura. "There was a prisoner that escaped from the downtown jail. There's a good possibility he was the one who stole your car. We have a notice out to all the cars in the area."

"Thank you, officer."

"I just can't figure out how he wired the car without the key."

Laura brought her hand to her lips. "Oh, I forgot. I had one of those key holders under the fender. I forgot all about it. Maybe he found it."

"Makes sense, now." He jotted something in his notepad and pulled out a business card. "Here's my card. On the back is a report number. You'll need it when you talk to your insurance. The report should be ready by the end of the day, and they can download it from our website. This number will get them started with a rental if you're covered."

"Thank you, officer. Yes, I'll need a rental. My grandmother's up north at the cottage and expecting me. I should be halfway there by now."

"Wait. What?"

"My grandmother. She's staying at our cottage. I'm going up as soon as I can get a rental."

Sgt. James squinted and scratched his head. "Maam. Laura. I don't want to alarm you, but do you have one of those nav consoles in your car?"

"Yes. Why?"

"Does it have the address of your cottage in it?"

"Yes. I always miss that one turn past Emsdale. Why…" Laura brought her hand to her lips again, her eyes widening. "Oh! You think he's gone there, don't you? Oh my." She pulled out her phone and dialed.

"Now we don't know that for sure, Laura." He held up his hands. "Chances are he's held up somewhere local. But just to be sure, I'll send it out." He turned away from her and spoke into his radio. "Dispatch… Yeah, it's James here. At the stolen car scene… Yep, that's right. I need a bolo put out on CPIC for the stolen car. License ABCD 555… Yes. To be apprehended right away. Also, can you have the OPP send a car to…" he motioned to Laura.

"426 Beaver Lake Lane." She was redialing but couldn't get through.

"To 426 Beaver Lake Lane outside Kearney… Yep. Tell them a possible escaped prisoner and to approach with caution. Send them the detail. Thanks."

"Approach with caution? What are you talking about?" Laura was trembling.

"It's just a precaution, Laura. It's being looked after."

"No, I need to be there," she screamed.

Kevin interjected. "I'll drive you up. Forget the rental. You're in no condition to drive, anyway." He looked at the sergeant. "Is that all, officer?"

"Yes. Please, don't approach if the police aren't there."

"Yeah, okay. Come on, Laura." She followed Kevin out to his car, hitting redial. She could not get through.

***

Maddie drew the last batch of cookies from the oven and placed them on the counter to cool. Six dozen chocolate chip as well as two dozen muffins. That should do the little rascal whenever he showed up. He was probably over at that gravel pit rooting through the rocks looking for treasure. That boy sure had an imagination.

She threw on the kettle and busied herself storing goodies in Tupperware containers until the water boiled. Five teabags went in the teapot, and she poured the water. She placed the teapot and a plate with six cookies on a tray and brought it to the stand, by her lazy boy. With a bit of an effort, she eased herself into the chair. A loon paddled back and forth on the lake about a hundred feet from shore. She nibbled on a cookie while the tea steeped. The stronger the better. She was about to pour her first cup when she heard a car door slam. That was odd. Laura must be early. She was trying to get out of the chair when the front door opened.

***

Tommy was polishing his gems when he thought he heard a car rolling down the Goldstein's half of the lane. He grabbed his binoculars and had a look. Yes. It was Laura's car coming up the drive. She parked at the side, not her usual spot. Someone got out but it didn't look like Laura.

The person was too big. Tommy adjusted the focus and zoomed in. It was a man. That was odd. Laura wasn't in the car either. It must have been some relative that borrowed her car. He racked his brain to figure out who it could be. Nobody came to mind. He'd better go check what was going on. He could call his mom from Maddie's.

***

Vince tried the door at the front of the cottage. Miraculously it was unlocked. *Rubes.* He was about to go back to the car and get his clothes and food when…

"Laura. Is that you?"

Vince froze. His mind went blank as he fought to regain some control. He hadn't expected anyone to be here.

"Laura? Stop your foolery, now. Come on in here. You're scaring me."

Vince's fight or flight responses kicked into overtime as he processed the situation. He was surprised that this lady expected someone this weekend. Probably the car owner. *Shit!* Not only was there someone here, but another was coming. He finally made a decision and walked in the door. "Hello, Ma'am," he called out. "I'm one of Laura's friends. She asked me to come up this weekend." He moved out of the small foyer into the open area of the cabin. A lone lady sat in a recliner looking over her right shoulder at him.

"Well, where's Laura? And who are you?"

"Laura's coming shortly. My name is Vince." He figured it wouldn't hurt to use his name.

"When? Where did she go?"

"She stopped to pick up some groceries. Should be along any minute." She was eyeing him now, sizing him up.

"What's that get-up you're in? Looks kind of silly, if you ask me, pardon my manners."

Vince glanced at his clothes, then shifted his left arm behind him. "I wore these 'cause Laura said we may be doing some hunting. It's the best I could find."

"What are you talking about? Laura's never hunted a day in her life. Wouldn't know which end of a rifle to hold. We don't even have a gun around here. Say, what's wrong with your arm? Mister, you're making me nervous. I'm going to have to ask you to wait outside." She pushed herself out of the chair. "I'm not comfortable with you in my house. Go on now."

Vince eased over to the fireplace and grabbed the poker, pointing it at her. "Sit down and be quiet. I don't want any trouble."

"You've got some nerve coming in here scaring an old woman. Why I..."

"Shut up!" He wavered the poker in front of her. "Now just sit down." He watched her plunk back into her chair. "Good, now stay there." He moved to the large window overlooking the lake and looked around. Everything was quiet outside, no sign of anyone. "Are you here alone?" he asked.

"Yes, Laura will be here soon, though."

Just one more thing he had to deal with. He struggled but was finally able to close the curtains. "We're going to have a quiet visit while I think."

Vince pondered his options. Leave. But to where? Stay here and wait for this Laura to come? One thing he didn't want was any more death and destruction. The lady was squirming again.

"It's too dark in here. Turn on a light."

"I said shut up!" He yelled.

She screamed.

***

OPP officer Nick Ramsey from the Burk's Falls detachment got the call at 16:45. He figured he was twenty minutes away, fifteen if he pushed it. The lights and siren went on as he headed south on highway 11 to 518. Two other cars were involved with a serious accident near Dunchurch so it would be just him for the time being. Proceed with caution was the order, and now a potential hostage. He pulled up the full report of this Vince character and hit "voice". An electronic voice spilled out the full report on the suspect's former arrest. Brutal. A tingle began at the base of Nick's spine and crawled up his back.

He was pulling onto highway 518 when his computer dinged. It was a preliminary coroner's report from the Barton Jail in Hamilton. Siri informed him in some gruesome details about the attack on the guard and inmates. Nick pondered how anyone could do so much damage by himself. Must be on some wicked drugs. He would need to be extra careful. He was getting closer and shut off the lights and siren.

Kearney came and went as he pulled into Beaver Lake Lane. Faded numbers were painted on wooden signs or family names announced the owners. Long twisted lanes led to buildings deep in the woods by the lake. Here it was. Goldstein/Anderson. The police car crept down the gravel lane. He stopped at a fork in the lane, around a hundred metres from the cottage, and got out. Signs indicated the Goldstein's to the left, Anderson's to the right. He crept down the left lane. A car matching the description stood at the side of the cottage. He was deciding whether to close in and match the plate or wait for backup when he heard the scream.

***

Tommy saw the police car driving up the lane before he got around to the back of the cottage. What was going on? Then he saw a flash of movement out of the corner of his eye. He checked with his binoculars. A man was looking out the cottage window overlooking the lake. Tommy hunkered down. The man scoured the area. Then he struggled with the curtains using only one arm. The other hung by his side. Tommy gasped, almost sucking in a leaf when he saw the fireplace poker in the man's hand.

The curtains were finally shut, and Tommy pondered. Something was wrong. Half running, half stooped, he scrambled over to the woodpile at the back of the cottage. A pile of logs lay close to a splitting trunk with an ax embedded in it. The entrance to the crawlspace was close by.

Tommy heard the scream, grabbed the ax, then wiggled under the crawlspace. His temples were thumping. He inched his way over to the trapdoor. Mrs. Goldstein needed his help.

***

Officer Nick Ramsey drew his weapon and ran to the front door. To hell with the backup. He would deal with any fallout later. Someone in there needed him. He eased the door open and cringed when it creaked. Around the corner, a voice called out.

"Who's there? Go back outside. Now!"

"Hello. It's Officer Ramsey from the OPP. Are you in there, Mrs. Goldstein?" He eased forward.

"She's here. Now leave."

"Is that you Vince? You know I can't leave. Let me hear from Mrs. Goldstein."

"I'm okay, officer." He heard a woman's shaky voice, then a dull thud and a scream.

"I told you to shut up." It was the man's voice. Nick swung around the wall and entered the large room, gun ready. A man stood over an elderly lady who was sitting in a recliner. Blood was oozing from her cheek. The man held a poker, raised, ready to strike again.

"Stop!" Nick had his gun trained on the man. "Drop the poker." This was a situation he trained for, but no matter what, a person is never truly ready. He held a steady gun, but this man was unpredictable. The man lowered it and placed the hook part against Mrs. Goldstein's throat.

"Don't be a hero. Just let me leave."

***

Kevin was pushing the car to 120 KM, but Laura thought they were standing still. Barrie's rush hour was over, and they were making good time. They were in Huntsville on the 11 and dodging nutbar drivers unaware of her situation. She had phoned half a hundred times and even used Kevin's phone but all she got was 'The Rogers customer you are trying to reach is unavailable…', maddening at the best of times, but infuriating now. With a concerted effort, she calmed herself down to a panic. Maddie was likely okay, humming, doing needlepoint while looking out over the lake.

No, she wasn't! Some homicidal maniac was gutting her like a fish, while she sat helplessly in this stupid car. Laura closed her eyes and slammed her fists on her thighs.

***

Tommy eased the trapdoor up, praying it did not squeak. After four inches of a gap, he encountered resistance. Something was laying on the door. He reached up and around to feel a cardboard box. His arm was not long enough to shove it off and his legs were beginning to cramp in their bent position. He grabbed the ax and lifted the trapdoor again, worked the heavy tool through the gap, and nudged the box aside. It thumped on the floor, and he grimaced, waiting for someone to come. His legs were on fire by the time he eased up onto the floor of the cottage.

The mudroom was small but functional. A "back" door, which led towards the lake, was behind him. A washer and dryer, a couple of boot trays, a small table, and a doorless closet completed the room. A short hallway led to the living room. He heard a man telling someone to not be a hero. Well, not him. Tommy was determined to rescue Mrs. Goldstein. He knew this was no game, though, as he snuck forward.

At the end of the hall, he stopped and glanced around the corner. A policeman was near the other door pointing a gun at a man beside Mrs. Goldstein. The other man was holding the fire poker to her neck, threatening her. The kitchen was to his right. Tommy pushed off the wall and ran towards the man, ax raised.

If Tommy had ever been to the mudroom before, he might have known about the squeaky floorboard at the entrance to the hallway. Things might have turned out differently. As it was, the living room soon became a scene of blood and screaming.

Officer Ramsey saw the flicker of movement as Tommy rounded the corner. He automatically trained his weapon on the new possible threat. Adrenaline flowed through him which caused an involuntary spasm of his trigger finger. His weapon fired.

Vince was deciding how to play this out when heard the creak of the floorboards behind him. He spun around, pulling the poker with him. It dug into Maddie's flesh under her chin and sliced a deep gash to her right ear. Blood began to pour. A small kid was running towards him with an ax. He raised his poker and advanced on the kid, then he heard the gun fire.

Tommy was around five feet from poker man when a searing pain shot through his right shoulder. He spun around and dropped the ax, his arm now useless. Through a blurry haze, he saw the man approach him swinging the poker. He managed to wriggle his head out of the way as the poker came crashing down, missing him by inches.

Horror ran through Officer Ramsey when he realized who he had shot. The poor boy lay there. He saw Vince advancing on the boy.

"Stop!" yelled the officer.

Vince saw the little punk's shoulder jolt as blood seeped into his shirt. Time to finish this off. He swung the poker, but the little bugger managed to wriggle out of the way. He raised it for another swing just before he felt a searing pain in his left side. Dropping to one knee, he heard the officer shouting.

The tingling began in the base of his spine and spread quickly throughout his body. Hair grew and his body parts changed. The pain was quickly forgotten. The transformation was happening.

Officer Ramsey saw Vince raise the poker a second time and fired. He was still shaking from hitting the boy and the bullet entered Vince's side. What happened next would haunt Nick for years to come. He planned to fire again, but his arm dropped to his side. Time seemed to stand still as he watched the changes. In some far-off place, he thought he heard Mrs. Goldstein scream.

The former Vince creature stood there, sneering. Long dangling arms, hands ending in claws, a long snout, saliva dripping from it and large incisors, ready to tear him apart. The creature looked around at Maddie and then towards him. It snarled and shook its head, shaking strings of saliva from its gaping maw.

Something snapped inside Nick. His job was to serve and protect. Whether it was instinct or training he didn't know, but his arm swung up and he fired two rounds into centre of mass. The creature pawed at the wounds and howled. It glared at Nick and advanced.

Tommy heard the howl and raised his head. Holy crap. That looked like something from one of his comic books. Like Wolfman. He struggled to his feet and wavered until his vision cleared. Maddie was slumped over in her chair, blood seeping from her chin. The ax lay on the floor, but it was too heavy to lift with one arm. It wouldn't work anyway. Nether would those bullets. Think! What killed the Wolfman in his comics? Silver bullets. But silver in general. Maddie's knife. The cool one. He struggled to the kitchen and grabbed it off the counter. Then he snuck up on the creature as it advanced on the policeman.

The creature leapt at Nick before he could get another shot off. He reached for his taser as the creature took a swing. A searing pain raged through Nick's left arm as he was flung to the floor. He managed to find his taser and fired. It stuck in the creature's chest, and it convulsed for a second. Then it reached up and yanked the wires out. It opened its mouth and was about to sink its teeth into Nick when it bolted upright and roared.

Tommy grasped the knife like a dagger and advanced on the creature. His hand and jaw quivered. He was hyperventilating and his heart raced. He vowed to die to protect Maddie and this policeman. The creature swatted the policeman aside. Tommy crept closer to the creature's back. He wasn't sure what he could do against this thing, but he would try. The creature stood upright and looked like it was vibrating. Tommy struggled forward, trying to run, trying not to jar his shoulder. With his left hand, he was able to sink the knife into the creatures back, just above its hips. It roared and swung its arms around. One of them struck Tommy's right shoulder and it exploded with pain. He passed out.

***

Laura grabbed the handle above her door as Kevin's car fishtailed down Beaver Lake Lane.

"There," she screamed, pointing. "That one."

The car careened into the lane to the cottage, then came to a screeching stop behind the police car. Laura jumped out and bounded to the cottage, Kevin closely behind.

She burst into the cottage, and it took a couple of seconds to register the scene. Her hand covered her mouth as she retched. Across the room, her grandmother slouched in a chair, blood down her chin and neck. To the right of Laura lay a police officer, blood all over his side. In front of her lay a man with a knife stuck in his back. To her left was Tommy, his shoulder also soaked in blood. Kevin bumped her as he entered the cottage.

"Whoa." His eyes flew open. "What a mess."

Laura looked between Tommy and her grandmother.

"Check out the boy," she said to Kevin and ran to her grandmother. Most of the damage was a tear along her cheek and jaw. She grabbed her cell phone to call 911. There was no reception. *Damn it.*

Maddie opened her mouth to speak, but only managed a weak groan. Her eyes were bulging, scanning the room. She motioned Laura away.

"Stay calm Grandma. I'm here. You're all right."

She saw Kevin cradling Tommy. The little boy screamed, and he almost slipped from Kevin's arms. His head jerked around.

"The monster. The monster."

Laura moved to his side. "There is no monster. Tommy, what happened here?"

"The monster. The axe. Policeman shot it…" He slumped in Kevin's arms.

She considered running to Tommy's cottage to use the land line. *No! Check the others, first.* The police officer began to stir. She ran to him. He looked at her, mumbling, then sat up alert.

"Get back. Get away. The creature." His eyes roamed the cottage, settling on the prone man. Then he saw Kevin. "Who's that?"

"A friend. He drove me here. I'm Laura, Mrs. Goldstein's granddaughter."

He seemed to relax and looked at her. Can you grab some towels and bring them here? We need to stop the bleeding. Call 911."

"I can't. No reception. Oh my God. Look at you."

"Never mind me. Just bring a towel and look after the others."

Laura ran to the mud room, almost spilling through the open trap door, collected several towels, and went to work controlling the bleeding on her grandmother while Kevin attended to Tommy. She wept continually.

Nick radioed the Muskoka Paramedic Services in Huntsville and explained the situation. Two ambulances were being sent from there and a third from Parry Sound. He busied himself stopping his bleeding as best he could and radioed dispatch. The shift supervisor was on his way.

Laura went next door to get Tommy's mother.

***

Laura walked into her grandmother's room in the Barrie Hospital. She was sharing it with Tommy, strictly against hospital protocol, but the stubborn lady had insisted and eventually got her way. Tommy was currently sleeping. Officer Nick was a couple of rooms down the hall. Laura still cringed at the sight of the bandages covering her grandmother's face. "Hello, Grandma. You're looking good."

Maddie raised her left hand and wavered it, the sign of so-so. She managed a raspy "Okay."

"I see you have your saviour with you. You are quite persuasive."

Maddie's left side of her face formed a brief smile, then she grimaced. "He's a good boy. Very sick, though. Like Officer Nick. Nice man. You would like him. He's cute."

"Who's cute?" a voice from the doorway inquired.

Laura spun around and saw a man standing there. His arm was in a sling and his shoulder bandaged.

"Laura," Maddie explained. "This is officer Nick. He and Tommy saved me from that horrible man. Devil man. Officer Nick, this is my granddaughter, Laura.

Laura got up to shake hands. *Oooh, he is cute*. Nick would have none of it and went in for a one-armed hug. "I've heard lots about you. All good by the way."

Laura blushed ever so slightly. Why thank you. And thanks for saving my grandmother, and Tommy."

He nodded towards Tommy. "I think it was him that saved me. I might have done more harm than good with him. His mother forgives me though." It was his turn to blush.

Tommy woke up and joined in, explaining everything again, in much greater detail than anyone else had managed, especially the monster. He was certain the man had turned into Wolfman. Monsters were real. It said so in his comic books. Laura shushed him and said he was imagining it. It was just a man. Vince had been pronounced dead at the scene, Tommy pronounced a foolish boy, but a hero, and Nick a poor shot. He was still under investigation but hoped he'd be cleared.

"We'll have to have you over for supper at the cottage in the spring," Laura offered him.

"I'd be happy to. Here's my card. My cell number is on the back."

She took the card and placed it in her clutch.

Ten minutes later a nurse came in and shooed Nick back to his room and took Tommy for some tests. Maddie motioned Laura over.

"There really was a monster there, you know. In the cottage. That man was a monster, he turned into one. A devil of a creature."

"Of course he was, Grandma. He did some terrible things. But he wasn't a real monster. Not like the ones I always thought were under my bed or hiding in the closet. Remember, the doctor said it was most likely Post Traumatic Stress Disorder. You didn't really see what you thought you saw. He was just a very bad man. Relax," Laura laughed, "It's not like he bit you and you're going to become a vampire or something."

Maddie patted her granddaughter's arm. "Of course not, dear."

MY SWEETHEART

Jimmy Carlisle tightened his tie and checked out the rest of his attire in the mirror. Good. Another run of the brush through his curly hair and he was ready. He walked over to his computer, logged out, grabbed his wallet and phone, and left his apartment. The outside stairs led down to the back yard of a two-story home. He rented the three hundred square-foot room above the garage on Toby Crescent. The late September day was comfortable as he strolled down a side street to Mohawk to catch the westbound bus.

He was off to see his girlfriend for lunch. She worked at Lime Ridge Mall at Melanie Lyne and ate her lunch in the mall food court. Jimmy often went to see her for lunch. He had a flexible work schedule which allowed him such liberties. Most of his work was online, helping security firms and web designing. He also did some computer repair.

Twenty minutes later he got off and entered the mall by the Fox and Fiddle. He was a bit early, and so he window-shopped at Henry's Camera Shop. The mall hadn't replaced the chairs or benches since Covid ended a year ago, so he couldn't sit. He checked his watch. It was about time to wander down the main section of the mall. He looked at some of the kiosks in the centre of the walkway, occasionally glancing toward Melanie Lyne's. He walked past the entrance and glanced in. She was not in sight; must be in the back. He strolled a little further, staring at window fronts until he headed back, passing Melanie Lyne's again. He looked but still did not see her, then wandered back towards Henry's.

Jimmy had been seeing Melissa for about 14 months now. He went everywhere with her: shopping, the movies, dinner dates, the beach; they'd even gone on a trip to Muskoka. She meant everything to him. They were taking it slow, though.

Jimmy remembered the first time he saw Melissa. It was a hot, muggy day in July last year. She needed a new computer set up, internet, email, the whole works. He'd spent an hour and a half at her place. That was when he knew she was the one. Her smile was infectious. It was a cliché but for him it was love at first sight. It was the beginning of a great relationship. She lived on the west mountain, near Bendamere and W19th Street. The topic hadn't really come up about them moving in together, let alone marriage, but he cherished their moments together.

There had been others of course, not all working out so well. Rachel in Saskatoon, with her long flowing red hair, a cute button of a nose, and that slightly husky voice. She was so adorable. He had gone everywhere with her as well. He eventually confessed his love to her, but the feeling had not been mutual, and a huge scene ensued. He could not figure out where he had gone wrong, and had left shortly thereafter, embarrassed. For several months he moped around and eventually moved to Brandon. There he found Charlotte and began a new friendship. She too was beautiful, and their relationship grew. He got to know her well and thought they were meant for each other, but again, when he confessed his love, she freaked out and he left, leaving him wondering what he had done wrong. He made his way to Hamilton where he had found Melissa, his true love.

Ah, there she was. As usual, dressed to the nines. Her curly, dirty-blond hair brushed the shoulders of her cream-coloured blouse, which was tucked into a navy-blue pencil skirt ending just below her knees. Practical flats covered her feet. She had a bounce to her step that stirred Jimmy's loins.

He followed her, keeping a safe distance. She hadn't noticed him, and he kept other shoppers between himself and her. It was a game he played—trying not to let her notice him. She walked down the aisle with

Jimmy always a two store-front distance behind. At the elevator, she turned right, towards the food court.

Melissa always got a chicken wrap from Timmies. Jimmy preferred Thai Express. He watched her progress through the lineup as he picked up a number 3 combo. That was his favourite, although number 4 was a close second. He waited until she was seated before he picked a strategic seat far enough away. It was a perfect line of sight for him to watch her.

She still hadn't seen him yet. He was getting good at this. Sometimes he could follow her for quite a while. It was like one of those detective shows, tailing someone. He liked watching her in her natural state, without his influence and either of them putting on airs. Of course, they spent intimate times together, but often he found this time intimate as well.

She unwrapped her sandwich and began to eat. He watched her chew her food. He brought out his phone and took the opportunity to snap several photos, zooming in on a few and made notes. Thirty-six. Twenty-seven. Thirty-four. Nice numbers. Oh, there was a nineteen and a twenty-two. Those were pretty good, but lower than the average. He kept track and had the numbers on a spreadsheet back home. The recommended number of chews before swallowing was thirty-two, but Melissa's average was well below - around twenty-seven. Still, Jimmy was not about to give her up because of that.

Melissa pulled out her phone and began texting. She watched for a bit then texted again. Jimmy opened an app called TextSee. It was one he had developed himself. A few seconds later he was reading Melissa's thread.

Melissa: *Wanta hit a movie?*

Tammy: *Not tonight. Groceries.*

Melissa: *Downer. Tomorrow?*

Tammy: *Sounds good. How's work?*

Melissa: *Same old. Done at 5. Bubble bath and Netflix, I guess.*

Tammy: *Have fun. Bye.*

Melissa: *Yeah, you too. Bye.*

So, she was staying in tonight. Jimmy would too, then. He looked forward to tonight and all the joy it would bring him. There was nothing better than date night.

She looked so beautiful he wanted to go up to her and confess his love but could not. It was better this way. He didn't want a repeat of the

Saskatoon incident, or the Brandon one for that matter. He had been hurt by each of those. Melissa was different, though. This was his true love. Nothing could come between them. He took a few more pictures and ate his own food while keeping track of Melissa's chew count. His was a perfect thirty-two.

She stood and placed her garbage in a receptacle and strolled down the mall aisle. Jimmy packed his leftovers and followed at a safe distance. She rounded the corner and he sped up and moved right behind her. He breathed in her scent, his favourite, while they walked as a couple down the aisle, he a foot or two behind. Her pace slowed and he stopped, focusing on the cell phone kiosk as she glanced back. She looked around, eyeing several people, smiled at him, then squinted. He dared not look directly at her but saw a quizzical look on her face out his peripheral vision; a look of trying to place someone. She eventually turned and carried on, entering Melanie Lyne. Jimmy was shaking. That was a bit too close, but worth it. She smelled so nice.

It was time to get back home, so he left the mall and caught the East Mohawk bus. Up in his apartment he logged into his computer and entered the data into his spreadsheet. There were several he kept on Melissa. Clothing, groceries, pay statements, movies she watched, television shows. He felt so close to her when he reread the information. They were such a great couple.

He busied himself with mundane work for the rest of the afternoon, security protocols, a new web page design, and a small emergency concerning a customer's database. At 4:30 he packed it in, contemplating whether he would join Melissa on her bus ride home this evening. He decided against it. Lunchtime's close call had left him spent. They would have to enjoy each other's company from afar tonight. He nuked his Thai and spent time cruising some dubious sites.

A ding came from his computer. Melisa was close to home. He clicked an icon and an image appeared on each of his four monitors, all different scenes of Melissa's apartment. During his first visit to install her computer, he'd been left pretty much on his own; she was outside doing gardening most of the time, so he decided to place two cameras. A month later he managed to enter her front door and spent most of the day installing better, high-definition cameras; swivel ones, hidden well. What a wonderful beginning to a beautiful relationship.

He had access to her computer as well, and therefore its contents, if he needed it. For the most part, though, he found the relationship strong enough that he stuck with the four main cameras. One for the living room/front entrance, one in the kitchen, the bathroom, and the bedroom.

She entered the front door at 5:47 and he recorded the time. He checked the GPS records on her phone and noticed she missed a bus connection. He loved the fact that she was so casual with her transportation, and chew count. He, with his accuracy, and she with her free spirit. They made such a great couple. She tossed her keys in the bowl by the front door and hung her jacket in the open closet. Soon she was on the kitchen camera preparing supper. Jimmy imagined her preparing meals for the both of them as he snuggled up behind her, smothering her in kisses. She finished and popped it in the oven. It looked like some sort of casserole. He made note of it, with all the contents and estimated quantities. It bothered him that he couldn't record the exact amounts but that would change once they were together.

It was back to the living room as she watched some PVR'd soaps. Jimmy didn't like her watching them because he got jealous of all the studs. Recently, however, he had begun downloading her PVR'd programs to his computer, inserting subliminal photos of himself strategically throughout, and uploading them back to her system. It was so romantic.

She paused the second show and removed the casserole from the oven. She opened a bottle of wine and poured a glass, bringing it and her plate back to the living room. He took note of her chew counts.

At 7:30 she drew her bath water and went to the bedroom to undress. Jimmy figured she had a nice enough body but could benefit from some sit-ups. Perhaps they could go to the gym someday. Bubble-baths usually took forty-seven minutes on average. Showers averaged seventeen minutes. Jimmy opened his email to check for any potential new clients. He didn't want to watch her bathe. There wasn't much to see. Besides, he thought it a bit creepy. A girl needs her privacy. He played a bit of Grand Theft Auto and waited.

Melissa grabbed a bag of chips and settled in for a Netflix movie. Jimmy didn't approve of her eating chips. Popcorn was better for her. He would send a Wellx message to her from her doctor reminding her of the disadvantages of potato chips, and junk food in general. She needed to stay healthy so they could be together forever. He loved looking after her.

The movie ended and Melissa headed to the bathroom. Jimmy noted her brushing numbers and followed her night routine until she was curled up under her blankets. He watched for several minutes until her breathing became regular. She was an angel, laying there. Jimmy reached for his mouse to shut the image down. He could watch it later. It was all being recorded.

Jimmy sighed. Things were going so great. It was time to take the next step. Tomorrow.

Good night my love. You are my sweetheart.

TOGETHER

Walter placed his arthritic toes into the saltwater of the Caribbean. He offered his arm to his wife, Edna. The waves were not bad today but sometimes the sand upset her balance. A strand of seaweed tickled his ankle as they moved further into the water.

He turned and smiled at his wife of 60 years. She smiled back and her face lit up, a radiance that warmed his heart and sent shivers through his body. Oh, he loved her so. They had managed to string together two weeks without doctor's appointments, tests, or bloodwork, and decided to come down to Punta Cana to celebrate their anniversary.

They were up to their mid-thighs and waves were breaking against them. He felt the undertow around his calves. Edna was wobbling.

"Shall we head back?" he asked.

"I think so, dear."

They headed to the pool. Jazzercise started at eleven. When he was younger, Walter would have played water volleyball at ten, but he wasn't 70 anymore.

Walter and Edna lounged around the pool all afternoon. At dinnertime they chose a romantic dinner at an a la carte restaurant. They ordered champagne, held hands, and reminisced about their wonderful years together. On the walk home, he took her in his arms, brushed a strand of white hair from her face, and kissed her. Later that evening, a glint of moonlight caught her eye as they lay in bed.

"Goodnight, my love," he told her.

"Goodnight, Walter."

He held his wonderful bride's hand as they drifted off to sleep.

Walter woke up in their bed at home. He often dreamt of the time in Punta Cana because it had been such a wonderful trip. He rolled over to kiss Edna, but she wasn't there. She must have got up early and grabbed a coffee. She did that a lot lately. He would find her out on the front porch.

I hope she put on a sweater. October mornings can get chilly.

He swung his feet out of bed and completed ten obligatory knee bends before he got dressed. His joints crackled like a popcorn machine. He worked his way down to the kitchen, his slippers not quite lifting off the floor, scraping the hardwood. Every couple of feet he reached out to the wall to steady himself.

The kitchen was a collage of mismatched colors. Turquoise-painted cupboards, faded orange wallpaper, and green appliances clashed with the squiggly red lines on the white table edged with a silver metal ring. David, their son, and his wife had tried to get them to update before they had passed on, but Edna liked it, so that was good enough for him. Only one chair was at the table. The fridge had large gold "Frigidaire" lettering. He walked to the coffee machine. It was one of those new-fangled ones, Kurtic or something like that. Beside the coffee machine was a faded yellow sticky-note.

Press Power Button to turn On
Place coffee pod in receptacle
Close lever
Place coffee cup on tray
Press "small" button
Wait for coffee
Press Power Button to turn Off

Poor Edna. She was becoming forgetful and did up notes like this to help her out. Walter turned on the small transistor radio and adjusted the antenna. Bryan Adams floated out the speaker asking the age-old question.

He smiled and nodded. Yes, he had loved a woman.

Walter made a cup of coffee, careful to follow the instructions on the note. After the last drop, he picked up his mug and headed down the long hall to the front door. He'd only made half a cup because he tended to shake a bit when he walked and spilled the coffee. Spaced equally apart, were the other three kitchen chairs and foldable TV trays. Walter had placed them there for Edna. Sometimes she got tired and needed a rest and a place to put her coffee. He stopped at the first chair and sat down. He leaned his elbow on the TV tray. These were certainly handy. There were only four left of the six. The fourth one was in the living room between their two recliners.

Walter glanced up at the wallpaper. Faded yellow over the years, it was a repeating scene of a horse-drawn sleigh. He remembered almost sixty years ago when Edna and he had put up this wallpaper. They had struggled and fussed and giggled and laughed. When they were finished, they stripped and made love on the floor right here in the hallway. Walter was sure they had conceived their son that day. David had grown up to be a fine lad, married well, and had his own son, Danny. David had been a firefighter. It was very sad what had happened.

Walter sipped his coffee, then eased up to a standing position. He stabilized himself, then moved forward. At the front foyer, he grabbed his coat, and stepped outside.

It was a wide porch, ten feet, and ran the length of the house. Robin-egg blue, with white, foot-wide columns every ten feet, and a white, wooden railing. To the right were two chairs where Edna and he watched the neighbors go about their business. All in all, it was a quiet street with little excitement. In the driveway was Walter's '67 Galaxie 500. The left front tire was getting low. Danny planned to pump it up the next time he came over.

Edna was not in her chair. Walter scanned the street. Maybe she had gone over to Martha and Ted's for tea. Boy, when the two of them got gabbing there was no stopping them. Ted was outside tinkering with that new leaf blower. Walter saw him through the bare branches of his maple tree.

"Hey Ted," he called out. "Is Edna over there?"

"No, Walter," Ted answered back, slowly shaking his head. "She's not. I'll be over later to blow your leaves."

"That's okay, Ted. Danny said he'll be over." Walter was proud of his grandson. Danny was a real cracker when it came to carpentry. Walter shuffled to his chair and noticed the porch floor was spongy. It had started last year in the far corner and was working its way across the porch. The eaves trough was leaking and dripping water onto the porch. The wood was getting softer with each rain. He almost fell through this summer and had to move the chairs further every month. Danny promised to come over to fix it, but Walter didn't know when. Danny was very busy these days. Walter hoped he would come soon because Edna liked sitting closer to the end of the porch where she got a better view of the neighbors.

Walter dragged his chair to more solid wood and sat down. Now, where was Edna? Had she gone to the corner store for something? Walter didn't like her doing that alone. He always went with her. Sometimes she had trouble counting the money. He didn't think the owner would take extra money from her, but sometimes there were hoodlums with skateboards and low pants hanging around outside. They called him Pops and her Ole Biddy. Not that he could do anything about it, but he felt he should be there to protect his wife. She would be okay at this time because those hoodlums never got up before noon.

Walter sat daydreaming about his son and daughter-in-law. It had been close to a year now, maybe more. A drunk driver had lost control and crashed into his son's vehicle. Both had died in the hospital. The drunk driver had walked away, unhurt. Danny had taken it hard. So had Edna. She hadn't talked for some time after the accident, but Walter eventually got her to speak. It had been a hard time for everyone. Maybe that was why Danny didn't come around as often. He wiped his eyes and sipped his coffee, staring into the street.

After some time, he headed back inside and placed his mug in the sink. He noticed the shopping list tacked on the fridge with a "Don't forget the butter" magnet. Just like Edna. Forgot the shopping list. She was doing that a lot more lately. He would need to have a talk with her about seeing Dr. Gilbert again. She hadn't seen him for close to a year now, maybe more. It was time.

Walter went to the bathroom to pee before settling into his recliner. He clicked the remote and got The Price is Right. They liked guessing the prices. Edna always got closer. He supposed that was because she shopped more than he did. This new guy was okay, he guessed, but Edna didn't like him. She preferred Bob Barker. She teased Walter, claiming Bob would be a good catch. He countered that she was only after his money. They always shared a laugh about it. This new guy had hosted another show, the one with the skits. Walter couldn't remember its name. The funniest episode was when that fitness guru, Richard somebody was on as a guest. Edna didn't like it because she thought it was too provocative. The Price is Right was over and Judge Judy came on next. Walter preferred Judge Alex, so he began to nod off.

Walter woke up an hour or so later. It was almost one-thirty. Where was Edna? By golly, she shouldn't be sleeping this late. He struggled out of his chair and shuffled down to the bedroom.

"Oh, there you are. It's late. Let's go for a walk. You should be up by now."

Edna smiled back but said nothing. Walter put a loving arm around her and kissed her.

"The sun is out. It'll do us good to get some fresh air. Come along." He guided her out of the bedroom and down the hall. "Mind the TV tables, now." Walter put on his coat, hat, and scarf. "There we go. We won't be long. Then we can watch TV together."

***

A jogger found Walter the next morning around seven. He was sitting, slouched over on a park bench. Freezing rain had formed icicles off the brow of his baseball cap. He was declared dead at the scene. He had a picture of his wife clutched in his arms.

Now they were together again.

YOUR SONG

This is a true story

Bob never considered himself a romantic. Sure, he bought flowers and gave cards for birthdays and anniversaries, but he wasn't the gushy type. That's why you may be surprised that he decided to serenade his wife with Elton John's "Your Song" for their tenth wedding anniversary. Did Bob know how to play the piano? Nope. Did he know how to carry a tune? Not if his life depended on it. That, however, would not deter Bob from carrying out his plan.

There's a couple of things you need to know about Bob. One, once a tiny seed of a thought takes root in his mind, it stays there. He takes on the challenge with tenacity, determination, and stubborn obsession, bordering psychosis. So, a little thing like not being able to play the piano or sing were minor obstacles that could be overcome.

The second thing about Bob is that he loves surprising people. From birthdays to unplanned trips, he takes great enjoyment in planning these undertakings. He prides himself in keeping them secret. His surprises were different than most. They were planned with all contingencies accounted for. He had surprised his wife on numerous occasions, small ones and significant ones.

However, with each additional surprise, came an increasing expectation for the next one. His wife was catching on to his methods and procedures. To pull off this particular surprise, he needed a complex plan, secrecy like no other, and precise execution, rivaling D-Day. Spread Sheets, Mission Statements, Executions Orders, and Contingency Plans were all thought through and written out.

It would be a three-phase operation. Phase 1: Acquire a keyboard and instructor and learn the song. Phase 2: Practice, Practice, Practice. Phase 3: Execute the surprise. It was July. He had 11 months to complete the task. Operation "Your Song" was a go!

Phase 1a. Acquiring the keyboard.

This was an easy part of the mission. Keyboards can be found in all the music and electronic stores. The hard part was to get it by the watchful eyes of Teresa, his wife. Bob had an office in the basement of their house, where Teresa hardly went. He knew it could be safely tucked away in there. The problem would be getting it from the car into the basement. The driveway at their house was situated by the side entrance to their home, but open to observation from the kitchen window, a place where his loving wife often spent time. He arrived at home from his purchasing excursion and went inside to determine where she was. She was not to be found. He hurried out the back and saw her leaving the side gate to go up the driveway. Surely she would see the huge box in the back of the SUV. Bob got her distracted by asking about relocating some of the perennials in the back. That dissuaded her from continuing. He sidetracked her for a while and then stole away to tuck his prized keyboard into the office. Later he unpacked it and hid the box behind the furnace. This part of the mission was complete.

Phase 1b. Acquiring the instructor

Bob needed to find an instructor. There were a few options for him to explore. He could find a home-based piano instructor and learn from them. He was not sure of that success as the instructor might want him to learn a bunch of basics before getting into the nitty-gritty of playing the song. His stepson was in a band and one of the members taught music. Perfect. Now, how was Bob going to contact this person? He didn't want to ask his stepson for the information. That would violate section 7 of the secrecy protocol for the mission. Bob knew the teacher worked for a company, but not which one. He would need to bide his time and wait for an opportunity. Meanwhile, he played the song over and over in his car, singing along, until he knew all the words. He thought he might even have sounded not too bad.

Bob decided to download the sheet music from the internet and try playing from those. There were a couple of problems with that. One was, he could not read music. He saw the five lines and the oddly shaped cursive S at the beginning. There were some 7's, lots of d's and p's, and a few b's, some of them filled in. He even saw a top hat. There were happy faces and sad faces joining all these together. He knew these were all some kind of notes, but this was pretty complicated. This would need to be simplified for him.

The second thing he realized was, it looked to him like these idiots on the internet might want him to play with more than two fingers at a time. Ridiculous. Bob was a beginner. He decided to try listening to someone playing while he watched the notes. His hands twisted into unreasonable positions no human should be required to duplicate. All manner of spasms and the onslaught of carpal tunnel syndrome began. This did not deter him. He was determined to succeed. However, in due time, he realized he needed some instruction. That was no problem. It was the middle of August. Ten months to go.

Then his fortune turned for the better. His stepson had a concert at the Zoetic Theater on Concession Street. Max, the instructor would be there. During a set break, Bob pulled Max to the side and swore him to secrecy. He considered having him sign a nondisclosure agreement, but decided against it. Then he described the situation and asked if Max could help him. It was agreed, and emails exchanged. The next day Bob contacted

Max and a time was set up for his first lesson. This part of the mission was complete.

Phase 1c. Learning the song.

The meeting was set for 7 PM, not a usual time for Bob to be out and about. To avoid suspicion, he needed a plausible reason to break his routine. He used the excuse that one of his friends needed help with his computer. That worked well, as he often helped friends with their computer woes. He had wrestled with the thought of fibbing but justified it as it would lead to a greater good. Bob arrived early, anticipating his first lesson. Knowing Bob's skill level, Max had simplified the music. First, Bob learned the individual notes for the song, their location on the keyboard and the length and rhythm. Max handed him some papers with the note locations and sent Bob home with the advice of lots of practice. He took it to heart and practiced at home as often as he could.

You may wonder how Bob practiced the piano without his wife hearing it. That was covered in Section 2, sub-para b, of the execution orders for the mission. He took his set of earphones and plugged them into the keyboard. Then he laid them down beside it. He set them loud enough so he could hear the piano through the headset, while still having an ear opened for his wife coming down the stairs. If he heard the creak of the stairs, operation "Fold Up" was executed. Unplug everything. Place the keyboard behind the desk out of sight. Music sheets, power cables, and earphones into the side drawer. Computer keyboard repositioned and a project ready on the computer screen. With a few trial runs this was accomplished in 30 seconds, loads of time before she arrived.

Bob needed a better ruse for heading out for lessons. There were only so many friends who needed computers fixed. Then he came upon a great idea. At the time, Bob was training to climb Mount Kilimanjaro by doing the Kenilworth steps. He utilized that time to go to Max's house and get lessons. He thought himself pretty smart until he got into the car to come home and realized he was not sweaty. He always came back sweaty after climbing the stairs. Coming back dry would arouse suspicion. So Bob turned his heater up full blast for the trip home. It was late August and a hot muggy day so the heat coming out was suffocating. When he arrived home, he was soaked. It worked as a good cover.

Bob eventually learned chords. The only others he knew about were the woodpile kind. He persevered and advanced to chord riffs. Then he tried his hand, or mouth, at singing while playing. He couldn't believe how much singing out loud threw his playing off so badly. He practiced singing at Max's house and whenever his wife was away from their home. Things were progressing slow but steady. It was Fall. Nine months to go.

Phase 2. Practice. Practice. Practice.

Bob practiced almost every day, into the Fall and December. I'd like to say he got good at it, but that would be stretching the truth. He knew the notes and worked on the rhythm, but it was hard to put it all together. As the weather got colder, Teresa spent less time in the garden, which meant less time to practice his voice. There was another hitch on the horizon. After Christmas, they would be traveling to Phoenix to winter for three months. He could not figure out how to bring the keyboard down there. It did not fit under the car seat. He figured he might need to get a second, smaller keyboard when they arrived.

Bob did get a smaller keyboard in Phoenix. It fit quite well under the seat. Most mornings he got up early and went to one of the many mountain preserves scattered throughout Phoenix. He spent an hour hiking and climbing and then returned to the car. He started it up, ran the air, and practiced on the keyboard. This went on for most days up until mid-March. That's when something drastic happened.

Now I must talk to you about the evilest of devices ever invented. Designed by demons, manufactured by the foulest of creatures, this device tears at the very fiber of your soul, crushing hopes and dreams, dashing away any semblance of self-esteem. Yes, of course, you know of it. I'm talking about a recording device. Like the camera sees everything, the recorder hears everything. Every quiver in the voice, every hesitation in chord changes, every replay of a note, every mistake, everything. It is designed to change the hopeful and mediocre, heard through our forgiving ears, into a barbaric assault on our senses. The recording device knows no bounds in its attack on our self-esteem. And so it happened to Bob. He recorded a practice session and played it back. It sounded horrible. Now he knew why the parking lot emptied so quickly when he set up. That's why the coyotes howled. His voice was horrible. What sounded so promising and good to his ears, changed drastically when heard back from the recorder. Bob was so taken aback from what he heard, he actually stopped practicing for several days. He eventually recovered from his shock and began anew. It played in the back of his mind, though. He knew he needed to step it up, and for the next two weeks worked extra hard. It was the end of March. Three months to go.

Teresa and Bob left Phoenix on March 31st and took three weeks to get home. They traveled through southern Utah, stopping at Zion, Bryce Canyon, and The Arches National Parks. Up to Wisconsin to visit friends, and then finally home. Bob was unable to practice during those three weeks. By the time they got home, Bob was itching to get back at it. There were two months to go.

May is the time to work on your garden. Too much, as far as Bob was concerned. Didn't his wife know he needed to practice? Of course, she didn't, so he helped with opening their pond, digging holes, planting annuals, preparing the lawn, and all the other spring outdoor chores. He did it with a smile, wishing he was downstairs tickling the ivories. Bob continued as the big day approached.

Phase 3. Execute the surprise.

D-Day had arrived. All the preparation, planning and secrecy would be over in an hour or two. Bob was nervous as the time approached. He and his wife were relaxing in the living room, or at least his wife was. It was around 11 AM. Bob was fidgeting and hyperventilating. It was time. He got up and casually, well as casually as he could, strolled into the kitchen. Now at this time, you must try to visualize the cartoon robber tiptoeing down the cellar stairs. You may even hear the steps descending the musical scale. Do, do, do, do, do, do, do, do, do. He raced over to his office and grabbed the keyboard and power cable. Back to the stairs. Now see the tiptoeing robber again, this time the sound going up the musical scale. Do, do, do, do, do, do, do, do, do. He took the keyboard into the dining room and set it up. Now down to get the music sheets.

"Bob, what are you up to?"

"Nothing." He tried his innocent voice. That usually didn't work.

"Well, that means you're up to something. Don't you think I know you by now?"

"It's nothing, you stay in there."

He scooted down to the basement and collected the music sheets, pausing for one last deep breath. Then up into the dining room. He set everything up and then walked into the living room.

"I have a surprise for you," he announced, the ever-present grin spread across his face.

"Oh, really. I never would have guessed." Teresa smiled.

"That's right, you'd never have guessed in a million years." he motioned to her. "Come with me."

Bob took Teresa's hand and led her into the dining room. She was taken aback by the keyboard and wondered what was going on. He asked her to be patient as he was not all that good, but this was a present to her for their tenth anniversary. Bob sat at the keyboard and felt the extra pressure of a live audience. He began to play. I'd like to say that his rendition went well and without a hitch, but that would be a lie. Let's just say it went okay. We have to face facts. Bob could not play the piano. Bob could not sing. What Bob could do, was try his hardest to give his wife a present she truly deserved.

MOUNTAIN MAN

This is a true story

I've always wanted to climb Mount Kilimanjaro. When I was a teenager, I vowed I would someday conquer this majestic mountain. I was at an age when false bravado could be claimed without any chance of being called on it. I learned about Africa in Social Studies, about Livingston and Stanley, and all the other explorers of the great continent, and I felt the sense of adventure, the lure, drawing me to it. Yes, I would make my way there; someday.

As with a lot of goals, though, life got in the way. High school, military, marriage, kids, career, and other hobbies all tried hard to break me from my teenage dream. I wouldn't say my desire left completely, it just took its own path, close enough to give me a quick wave every now and then, but too far away to stay in the forefront of my mind. Maybe my dream took time to climb the mountain itself, in preparation.

Fast forward to Jan 2014. I had retired from my second career seven months before and my wife and I were going to Phoenix for six weeks to escape the winter and soak up some sunshine. We enjoyed hiking and sought out different trails around the area. The city has many mountain preserves, and we began exploring them. They are not real mountains, the ones within the city are two or three hundred feet high, except for Camelback Mountain, a 1,400-foot elevation gain.

When I first set eyes on Camelback, a little tingle formed inside me. I wasn't aware of it at the time, but that was when my dream turned a corner and started heading back to me. My wife and I continued our hikes, gaining strength and endurance. In the back of my mind, Camelback was always there, smiling, beckoning me.

My niece, Debbie, and her husband, Jim were down in Phoenix too. We did several things with them, one of which was driving the Apache Trail. At every pull off we got out and climbed rocks, admired the scenery, and enjoyed nature. It might have been here that my dream finally got through to me, still from afar, but I heard it.

Jim and I made arrangements to climb Camelback. The girls were going shopping. They dropped us at the eastern trail, and we began our ascent. The eastern trail was longer but an easier climb. I felt the heat of the Arizona sun beating down as my pace began to slow. The open landscape provided little shade. After half an hour it was clear I was slowing us down. My heart rate was high, and I was out of breath. We were resting too often. Behind us were three nuns in their habits, enjoying a nice stroll. I said to Jim there was no way we were letting some seventy-year-old nuns pass us.

Fifteen minutes later, we were eating their dust.

The effort to stay ahead of them had done me in. My heart was racing, and I was wheezing like a locomotive. We rested for half an hour before I felt I could move on. And move on we did, for another two hours, before we finally made it to a saddle. So far, we had been walking on a trail, no rock scrambling. Before we began the serious climbing, steep and narrow, we contemplated continuing. I wasn't sure I would make it back down. I have a fear of heights. Going up wouldn't be too bad, but coming down was different. So, with dwindling water, time against us, exhaustion, and my indecision, we headed down the hill. We had gotten halfway by distance, one-third of the way by elevation. We vowed to seek revenge.

The Camelback experience taught me a couple of things, one of them being I was out of shape. I was fine doing a quick climb up a hundred feet, but I would need sustained climbing to help my cardio and I needed cardio to do sustained climbing. I couldn't run because I had a bum knee, so it was climbing or nothing.

In our last week in Phoenix, we found a mountain preserve that had a nice climbing mountain called Lookout. It had a 500-foot elevation gain and two approaches. There were three other good-sized hills we could hike over as well. I went three-quarters of the way up Lookout a couple of times, before we headed back home, promising to get to the top next year.

During the summer of 2014, I continued my hiking and started doing stairs on the escarpment. Between those and the hills in the King's Forest, I maintained some semblance of cardio training. I bought a water camel and better hiking boots. My dream was whispering louder to me, and I started talking about Kilimanjaro to my friends, putting out feelers you might say. Some took it as a joke, while others supported it. I began researching tours and what I would need to do to accomplish my goal, though it was still a distant dream.

My wife bought me a book about Kilimanjaro for Christmas, the dos and don'ts, what to expect, the different routes with detailed explanations. She also had an urge to see Africa. She had done a project on it in grade school and told her teacher one day she would go there. We began gathering information for a trip. My dream knew it could come back; and it did, enveloping me, making me stronger. Now I wanted to climb Kilimanjaro. It was no longer a wispy statement made as a teenager long ago. There was a drive and determination to do it. I hadn't actually made the decision I was going, but I was damned determined to give myself the best possible chance to make it if I did.

We left for Phoenix on Dec 28th for a three-month stay. During this time, we had both decided to eat healthier and lose some weight. When we got to Phoenix, I went to Lookout mountain every morning early, before my wife got up. It took me five tries of lumbering up the trail before I finally made it to the top. The first time it took me one hour and twenty minutes to get to the top, with several breaks. I thought I'd done well. At the end of three months, it took me twenty-two minutes and no stops to get to the top.

After I came back from doing Lookout, we would have breakfast and go out for a hike together. Don't think it was all work and no play. We spent afternoons at the pool soaking up the sun. We also managed to lose over one hundred pounds between us and were in pretty good shape. Around two months into our vacation, I tackled Camelback, this time from the west, and made it to the top. I was filled with euphoria and if this was what summiting felt like, I wanted more. I'm pretty sure that's when I knew I could do Kilimanjaro.

We had been talking about going to Africa and doing a safari, so now I would be adding a climb up the mountain to that. When we got back home, we were blessed with our first grandson and got ourselves sidetracked. We eventually made it to a travel agent and gave her our wish list. We couldn't decide on a date. The best time to go is in the fall, or spring, during the dry periods. We finally decided on the fall, but it was now too late to book for this year. For the remainder of 2015, I kept hiking King's Forest and doing the escarpment stairs.

In 2016 we wintered in Phoenix from January to March. We continued hiking and I often climbed Lookout twice, and a few times I tackled it three times. I was trying to simulate climbing for eight hours, with 3,000-foot elevation gains, something I would encounter on Kili, but couldn't accurately simulate it here.

One of my friends from Hamilton over-winters in Gold Canyon and runs a hiking group for her trailer park. It takes around an hour and a half to get there, so for most hikes, I didn't bother going. For their grand finale of the season, they always did Flatiron, a ten-kilometer, 2,800-foot elevation gain grind to a beautiful view of the valley. I gladly signed on as this would be a perfect test for me. We started at eight o'clock and began on a meandering gentle meadow slope. Then it was pure, one hundred percent effort, with little time for rest. Although we had the whole day, it would take longer to come down than to climb, so we pushed onward. Sometime around noon we broke through onto the short trail leading to a large flat rock formation that looked like—you guessed it—an upside-down iron. There was a short break for lunch, pictures, and videos. Some climbers had their pictures taken near the edge, but I stayed well enough away. Soon we started the long journey down. At least the trail was gradual enough that my fear of heights never kicked in. I arrived at my car around six, exhausted, but feeling good. Over 30,000 steps and around 7,000 calories burned. Nothing was stopping me now. I was going to the top of that mountain.

We booked the vacation to Africa, and I spent most of the summer of 2016 hiking and climbing stairs. I read in my book that the more you trained before the attempt, the more you would enjoy the attempt, so I put everything I had into training that summer and early fall. I stopped two weeks before my flight to allow my body to recuperate.

There are five main routes up to the peak of Kilimanjaro, each with its pros and cons. I chose the *Machame* route for a couple of reasons: First, it had the highest success rate of all the routes, because it is the longest and allowed for better acclimatization to altitude. The second, and more important for me, was the option to take an extra day, which would spread out the forty-kilometer hike. The downside of the route was it is the hardest because of its length.

The day finally arrived. I was leaving ten days before my wife and completing the climb before she joined me for a safari. It took two days to finally arrive at a basic need's hotel with spotty Wi-Fi. I spent the next day relaxing and getting over any jet lag while repacking all my gear and steeling myself for the climb.

I had intended to pick up a SIM card to keep in touch on the mountain, but returning climbers said the reception was iffy. I met a group of Germans and a British guy living in Indonesia who were climbing the next day as well as I, although with different groups. I sat and had drinks with the Germans and practiced my limited use of their language. I would see them a lot in the next week.

During the day the huge mountain could be spotted through a gap in the trees, its presence reminding me what was in store. It is hard to understand the size of Kilimanjaro until you are there. It is comprised of three volcanos, Shira, at 13,150 feet, Mawenzi at 16,893 feet, and Kibo at 19,341 feet. These mountain "peaks", actually craters, are twenty-four kilometers apart, so you can imagine its diameter at the base. Because of its size, there is no rock climbing involved and little rock scrambling. Ninety-five percent of the climb is on a trail.

From ten kilometers away it loomed over me, challenging me to come and conquer it. I was nervous but confident. I had studied every step of the route and knew what I was up against but standing in its shadow (figuratively) I could almost hear my dream whisper; *Careful what you wish for*.

Day 1

My guide and porters arrived around eight o'clock the next day. They moved with great efficiency and had everything packed within the hour. There were five porters, one cook, and a guide, seven people, just for me. I felt like one of those British explorers from the 1800's, Stanley or Livingston. Introductions were made and I had trouble remembering all their names, except my guide, Ernest. They christened me *Babu*, which means Grandpa in Swahili.

I had ordered a cot to sleep on and a larger tent that I could stand up in-- after a long day of climbing there would be no crawling in and out of tents for me. The porters would take up to twenty kilos of personal gear and the rest was my responsibility. They carried tents and sleeping bags, food for all for eight days, propane, water, and who knows what else. I carried my water camel, a few snacks, and a change of socks.

We piled into a van and drove the hour to the Machame Gate. The gate consisted of a huge parking lot filled with vans. There were several pavilions for hikers to congregate. Several administrative buildings hurried the signing-in process. There were hundreds of guests all waiting for the red tape, each with four or five guides and porters each. The place was swarming with people. I found the British hiker that had stayed in the same hotel as mine and we talked for a while.[1]

Ernest rounded me up, I signed in and stood by the gate awaiting my first actual step on this crazy journey. Without much fanfare and nary a photo, I started my trek up the tallest mountain in Africa. The first forty-five minutes or so was a gentle climb along a four-wheel-drive road. Nervous energy had me walking at a brisk pace, but Ernest kept calling out *Polepole* in Swahili, which means 'slow'. I would hear this at least one hundred times in the next six days. The guides wanted their guests to go slow to get used to the elevation gain. Most failures occurred with people that went too quickly and usually got into trouble with altitude sickness. Slow and steady wins this race, a fact I was well aware of and glad for. I didn't care how much training I had done, there were sixty-year-old parts involved in this endeavor.

[1] Every porter and guide had to be checked out by the park officials to see if they wore proper boots and each of their packs were weighed to ensure they were not overburdened. In the past, tour companies would send porters up the mountain in flip-flops and limited clothing, endangering them. Rules had been put into place to protect the porters and were strictly enforced.

The road gave way to a single file, steeper path through a dense forest with large ferns and the sprinkling of Kilimanjaro Impatiens. The lush forest smelt earthy. Birds chirped and an occasional squawk of a distant parrot penetrated the tall trees. Ernest pointed out and named some of the vegetation, but for the most part, I was concentrating on the hike.

Three hours into the trek, my porters went motoring by with the greeting of *Babu*. There was no *Polepole* for them as they scurried up the path to get to camp and set up my tent and cook supper. I watched them with their own personal kit for the trip plus an additional 20-30 kilos of provisions. Some of them carried over half their weight. I felt sorry for them but did not offer to relieve them of any load. They were used to the altitude and made the climb 20 times a year. My guide, Ernest had summited 317 times in his seventeen-year career.

We took a break every hour which I very much appreciated. Today's trek was eleven kilometers long, with a 3415-foot elevation gain. At one o'clock we stopped for lunch. Hundreds of trekkers sat on stumps and logs eating their prepared lunches. I saw my German friends from the hotel, and we exchanged pleasantries. Then we packed up and continued our climb.

The forest began to thin, making way to moorland, grasses, and better views. With only an hour left we finally broke through the canopy into open, rolling hills, shrubs, and grasslands. The earthy smell of the forest was replaced by the slight grassy smell and the occasional whiff of food cooking. The forest was below, the rocky mountain crags above, and the misty clouds surrounded us. I was feeling pretty good, considering, and my spirits were high, buoyed further when we rounded a corner and the Machame tent-city stood before me. Hundreds of different coloured tents were strewn over a couple of acres of relatively flat land. My porters (I felt odd calling them that) were waiting by the camp sign and did a short welcoming song and dance. I dropped my pack in my tent and signed in at the ranger station. When I returned to my tent, a basin of hot water and soap was waiting for me. My cot and sleeping bag were already laid out, my extra kit stowed in the tent, and some fresh fruit waited in a basket. I scrubbed up, checked my feet for blisters, then went outside to take some pictures and a few videos. Hundreds of tents of various sizes, shapes, and colours were strewn about, logos of the numerous tour companies etched into the fabric. Kilimanjaro loomed in the distance.

My supper arrived shortly after. They had set up an extra tent for dining with a tablecloth, lots of condiments, a thermos with hot water, and packets of chocolate energy drink. There was a huge tureen of Hungarian Goulash. I wolfed two bowls of that down with bread and thought 'not bad', not knowing what to expect for meals. At least it was hot. My 'server' came to take the empty dishes and said 'two minutes'. In less than that he returned with the rest of the meal. I could not believe my eyes. There was an oval serving platter with breaded cutlets, at least six, and another serving platter with rice mixed with vegetables, enough for four people. Rounding off the meal was a plate of breaded plantains. I looked at him, then the food.

"You must eat all. Make good energy. Ernest come. Check on you. Eat."

Now, I love a good meal and I can pack my fair share away, but this was going to be a challenge. I managed to get four cutlets down and half the rice when Ernest showed up. I was full, stuffed actually, and could eat no more. I was never hungry for the whole trip.

He was concerned I hadn't finished, but I ensured him I'd had enough. One of the symptoms of altitude sickness was loss of appetite, so he was keeping a close look at everything I ate. This would become a daily routine, his checking up on my eating habits, asking questions about how I felt, and keeping a close eye on me during the trek. I felt like I was in good hands.

I went outside and took some more photos and stared at the peak, still several kilometers away. I checked my Fitbit. Over 28,000 steps, 4,000 feet of total elevation gain, and 6,000 calories burned. The sun was setting, and the cold was moving in. I retired to my tent. Day 1 on the mountain had come to an end.

Day 2

I slept well through the night, being absolutely exhausted, and woke to the hustle and bustle of the morning camp routine. I was up and dressed before Ernest came to wake me. Breakfast was huge and I ate most of it. A quick repacking of my kit and I was ready to go. Water had been boiled for my camel and I added some energy-mix powder to it.

Today, there would be more rock scrambling than Day 1, with a 5-kilometer hike, 3,020-foot elevation gain to a height of 12,375 feet. We were in the Moorland vegetation zone comprising of open slopes of short windswept evergreen shrubs, and lots of grasses. Rock outcroppings dominated the landscape. We ascended through the layer of clouds, moisture clinging to our gear. Once through, I felt the warmth of the sun as it forced the clouds into the valleys. At a rest stop, I looked back and saw the Machame Campsite, now a tiny postage stamp scar amongst the vegetation. We were climbing almost the same height today as yesterday, but in half the distance, so it was much steeper. Lots of stops and picture taking and the never-ending *Polepole.* I will admit, it was exhausting and welcomed every stop for a rest, under the guise of taking a picture. My porters passed me and scooted up the path like mountain goats. *Hey, Babu.*

The mountain peak loomed to the right, egging me on, teasing me. With thirty kilometers still to go, I was starting to wonder if I would make it. Little seeds of doubt blossomed in amongst my stubbornness and determination. I shook them aside to focus on today's trip and would worry about tomorrow in the morning. Eventually, we reached the halfway point and stopped for lunch. I saw my German friends and my spirits lifted. After an hour we started up the slope again.

I was feeling good, besides the aching muscles and heavy breathing, and had no headaches, nausea, or other symptoms of altitude sickness. My feet were not blistering, and I had no raw areas on my shoulders or lower back, usual hot spots for carrying a backpack. Hundreds of hours of preparation for this trip were paying off. I remembered the words of wisdom; train before you go, so you can enjoy the climb when you get there.

Shira Cave Camp soon came into view and the sight of my tent was most welcoming. I washed up and had another huge supper. After Ernest's daily checkup, I went outside and took more pictures. Kilimanjaro loomed to the east, the sun casting its last rays on it before it set. Mount Meru sat to the west, the sun beginning to set behind its peak. It cast a halo effect as it inched its way down. Much closer was the 13,140-foot Shira Mountain, more a ridge than a peak. There were caves nearby to explore, but I didn't want to waste any energy climbing up to them so with the daylight fading, I retired for the night, knowing what was in store for me tomorrow.

Day 3

The next morning was the same routine. Hearty breakfast, repack, and start our hike. Day 3 is an acclimatization day with a 10-kilometer, 2,805-foot climb to 15,180 feet, and then descend 2,310 feet into Baranco Camp. The reason for this is to check out the climbers to see how they are affected by the altitude. If needed, they can be taken down the mountain from the Baranco Camp. At this time, we were west of the peak, traveling east around the southern base of the peak for three more days until we made the final ascent from the southeast.

We head up into the Alpine Desert vegetation zone, but in reality, there is little vegetation. It looks like the Arizona desert I trained in for many kilometers. The sun was unrelenting with no shade for relief. We rested by rock outcroppings, where we huddled together in their shadows. I had a water camel and two other water bottles full, and I was going to need them. With such an open area where you could see long distances, I became weary each time we crested another ridge and saw our lunch stop far in the distance. I began to wish for the lush forest, for its shade and trail secrets. I had momentary breaks when I met my German friends and was greeted by numerous porters as they motored by.

We arrived at Lava Tower, which is a volcanic plug some hundred feet high, for lunch and welcomed the sit-down in the shade. Ernest was checking me over very closely. I had no symptoms of altitude sickness, or attitude sickness, for that matter. A daily dose of Diamox, prescribed by my doctor, helped alleviate those symptoms. I was feeling pretty good, actually. Don't get me wrong, I was tired, my muscles ached, and my feet were a little sore, although still no hot spots. I had a good look at the mountain looming in front of me. We were closer to the peak here than we would be when we started the final ascent, but the route up was treacherous and required serious mountain climbing skills.

With a final wave goodbye to Lava Tower, we began our 2,300-foot descent into Baranco Camp. My knees don't like going downhill and the three kilometers took as long as the last seven of climbing. It was getting late in the day and Ernest was urging me along. No more *Polepole* now. He asked if I had my headlamp with me and that got me thinking how far we had to go. Two porters showed up and a rapid exchange of Swahili happened before one headed back, I suspect with a time of our arrival, while the other one walked with us.

We arrived before nightfall, in fact, we had an hour to spare, but it left little time to register, get cleaned, and eat before darkness. My foot check and exchange of clothes were done by flashlight. Day 3 ended with early retirement and a night of deep sleep.

Day 4

The Baranco Wall. I was looking forward to this day. An 800-foot rock scramble up a steep cliff. It was a welcome change from the endless kilometers of trails and *Polepole.* I was out of my tent early to take photos I wasn't able to yesterday.

After a hearty breakfast and packing my gear, we headed off to conquer the wall. No hiking poles for this portion of the trip, just gloves, and sure feet. My only concern was my fear of heights. Would I freeze halfway up? I was thankful that I needed to concentrate on foot and hand placement and that I was facing the wall for the most part. It was all rock scrambling and not rock climbing, the difference being I was always on a trail of some sort and never had to pull myself up or dangle by a fingertip, struggling for a toehold. Frequently I needed to steady myself as I shifted from one rock to another, but I never felt at risk during the ascent. The hardest part was going around Kissing Rock, about halfway up. It is a large boulder that sticks out onto the pathway, with a significant drop off the edge. Ernest took my backpack while he and another person supported my back as I hugged the huge boulder and inched my way around it. My adrenalin was flowing, and I think I peed a little. We made several stops going up for rests and picture taking. There were lots of choke points along the way and it soon became like a traffic jam during rush hour when the stream of porters arrived.

After a couple of hours, we reached the top and had a well-deserved rest. Mount Meru stood farther to the west and Kili, ever-present, loomed to the north. After a few pictures and a snack, we were on our way.

I passed my German friends and exchanged boisterous greetings. It may sound like they were the only ones on the trail, but there were many. Every day I passed many other trekkers and bonds were formed. We would leapfrog each other several times a day, as they stopped for rests, then I. There was an American gentleman and his grandson, or very young son, who always had encouraging words. The man was easily in his seventies and was on oxygen. His companion, grandson or son, was in his late twenties.

With the excitement of the wall over with, we settled into *Polepole* along dusty trails and barren landscape. We traversed a couple of valleys, trudging down the trail to the floor, crossing a tiny trickle of a stream, then up the numerous switchbacks to the other side, only to do it a kilometer later.[2]

Finally, I spotted tents in the distance. Out came my camera and I zoomed in. Yes. They were only about a kilometer away and it was around three o'clock. Karanga Camp. I was grinning, but when I looked at Ernest, he was waving his finger with a look on his face that had me worried. No, no, no, he was saying. He motioned to carry on. Twenty minutes later I saw what he meant.

Between us and the camp was the huge Karanga Valley. Eight hundred feet down, and of course eight hundred feet up the other side. Couldn't they have built a bridge? With my fear of heights, I wouldn't have crossed it, but hey, at least give me a choice. With somewhat dejected enthusiasm I started down the endless path to nowhere, deeper and deeper into the bowels of hell, only to find real hell on the climb back up. My knees were on fire during the descent and did not get better on the climb. The sun was a relentless, energy-sapping demon, crushing my enthusiasm. Three hours from that joyful moment when I first spotted the camp, I signed into the ranger station and flopped on my cot for a fifteen-minute rest before my washing water arrived. Once I had the dirt scrubbed off, I felt better and sat down for my monster meal. My friend from the hotel stopped by and asked if I wanted to send an email back home to my wife. He had an old analog phone, so I kept my message short, saying I was doing well and would see her in a couple of days. A message came back later, and the guy swung around to my tent again to let me read it. I sent another short email back. Back home, my wife was

[2] This two-day stretch was one of the reasons I chose this route. It afforded me an extra day on the mountain for acclimatization. More importantly, the company I chose advanced to an intermediary camp. Most companies stayed at Baranco Camp for an extra day but then trekked thirteen kilometers to base camp. Shah, the company I used, advanced nine kilometers to Karanga Camp today, leaving only four kilometers to travel to base camp the next day before summitting. This was important for me because it would allow me to arrive at base camp around noon, instead of six or seven at night, then leave for the summit at midnight.

wondering why the emails were so short and I wasn't explaining the trip to her, but I was getting frustrated with the keyboard. I had time to take one picture of the sun setting beside Mount Meru, now in the far distance. Although we had only made a 300-foot elevation gain, I figured I'd climbed around 3,000 feet today in total, so I welcomed my cot and bedroll and fell fast asleep.

Day 5

Today was a short day in comparison to some of the others. Four kilometers distance and a 2,225-foot elevation gain. That didn't mean it was any easier, though. At 14,000 ft I was puffing air and moving slow. I took *Polepole* to heart as we trudged along the path, the mountain in plain view to my front left.[3]

The landscape was an absolute rock desert. There was not one plant in sight, just endless kilometers of open plains of volcanic rock. Dusty, gray boulders with the occasional black volcanic ridge in the distance. Gritty, aquarium-sized pebbles, crunched as I trudged along, methodically placing one foot in front of the other. I could see the countless hikers ahead and behind me, all striving to achieve the same goal. We looked like zombies, slowly marching to our end. My cook joined us for a bit, and we got some pictures. Mostly though, today was placing one foot in front of the other, a robotic activity with seemingly no end. Greetings from other hikers were less joyous as the monotony of the barren landscape and drudgery of the hike set in.

We forged along and came to a crest in the path. In front of me lay one last shallow valley with a steep ridge on the far side. With a huge sigh, I started my descent. I could see the hundreds of hikers in line marching along the valley before me. There were many more behind.

---

[3] The porters had to work extra hard during this portion of the trip. There was no source of water at the next camp. There were barrels and collection roofs for when it rained but the barrels would be empty during this dry season. The closest water point was at the bottom of the 800-foot valley I climbed yesterday. Upon arrival, the porters had to climb down and collect water for supper. Then they had to go down again to bring up water for breakfast. Then after breakfast, go down again to haul water to the next camp. Once they arrived at the base camp, they had to travel back to this last camp, climb down, gather more water, and take it back. Four times down and up the valley. All the water needed to be boiled before use.

We eventually reached the other side and topped the ridge. The path split in two here with a sharp left turn heading up to Barafu Camp, our destination for the day, and the other heading down the mountain to Mweka, the exit route. There was a steady stream of hikers, who had made the summit attempt last night, coming towards us as we ascended. Every now and then I spotted a downcast face amongst the endless crowds, a clear indication of defeat. It was disheartening; gut-wrenching, actually. I began to look down to avoid those sad faces, something you should never do. Looking down saps your energy as well. My feet became heavier and true doubt seeped in, elbowing my dream aside.

I saw my German friends coming down the path. They were not their usual boisterous selves. They were surprised I was heading up the mountain. They had not chosen the extra day and had walked the extra distance yesterday and attempted the summit last night. I asked how they did. Only six of the thirteen had made it, some failing from fatigue, some from the cold. They had not come prepared for the bitter cold of the ascent in the dark. I was devastated by their numbers and said I would see them at the hotel. We would have a drink. I never saw them again. They were gone when I got back to the hotel.

Somehow, in some twisted way, meeting the Germans lifted my spirits. I had taken the extra day; they had not. I had all the proper clothing for the ascent; some of them had not. It tugged on my soul that I was using their misfortune to buoy my spirits, but at that point, I needed it.

We arrived at Barafu Camp around noon, 15,331 feet. After signing in and taking the obligatory picture of me at the sign, I collapsed on my cot, exhausted. I did not move for quite some time. Lunch came and I wolfed it all, then lay back down. I took a video of the inside of my tent from the prone position and called it Lazy Video. The wind picked up dramatically and the tent was flapping like crazy.

Ernest came to check on me, including what I would be wearing tonight. I showed him all my clothing and he was happy. He said it would be cold. The wind would be around 40 KPH and the temperature around -15 C. That put the wind chill at close to -30 C. In Africa? He left me to ponder those facts as he went about his own business. I'm not a stranger to the cold, I spent three years in Shilo Manitoba, where -30 C could be considered a warm spell. And that's without the wind chill. However, living through it does not make it better. It still sucks being cold.

I finally mustered the energy to drag myself out of bed and take some pictures of the mountain and a video or two. Late-comers were still coming down the path from the peak. In twenty-four hours or so I would be doing the same, hopefully with a skip in my step.

Tomorrow would be a long day. The plan was to start at midnight and begin climbing, with the idea of reaching the summit at sunrise. Then back down to this camp for noon and lunch. Then another walk to the Mweka Camp before supper. So, tomorrow would include a total of 16.5 kilometers, 5 climbing, and 11.5 descending. Elevation-wise, it was a 4,009-foot climb and a 9,137-foot descent. It takes five and a half days to summit and a day and a half to descend.

Supper came and I managed to eat it all. Ernest stopped by for one last check and gave me the okay. I prepared my clothes for the midnight start. I expected to shed layers as the sun rose and it warmed up. There were four layers for my legs and five for my body. Two pairs of thick socks and a pair of boots half a size larger to accommodate them. Thick gloves, a balaclava, a hooded jacket, three headlamps, and two flashlights rounded out my ensemble. I assembled them in a semicircle around my cot so they could be quickly put on in the freezing dark. I had even practiced a couple of nights ago, in the dark.

As you may, or may not know, when it's bitterly cold and you are sleeping in a proper, winter sleeping bag, you should not sleep with any clothes on. There are two reasons for that: One is that you will be warmer without your clothes. Heat from your body will disperse in the bag and help keep low heat-producing areas like your toes, warmer. If you wear socks your feet cannot benefit from the higher heat-producing body parts. Second, if you wear clothes in the sleeping bag, they will become damp from sweat and will be a liability when you awake and expose yourself to the cold. Damp clothing does not insulate well. That is why all my clothes were laid out in specific order ready to be put on quickly. Yes, for the first minute or so you may be doing the *freezing-two-step* until you have enough layers on, but you will benefit in the long run.

With my clothes laid out, I went to sleep around seven waiting for my wake-up call.

Summit Day

I had a decent sleep even though the tent was flapping with the wind. Ernest woke me up at 11:30. I jumped out of bed and did the *freezing-two-step* until I had a couple of layers on. At least inside the tent, I didn't have to deal with the wind chill but -15 C is still cold. I ate a bowl of soup and prepared myself for the final leg of my journey.

I felt good physically. At this altitude, I had to occasionally force a deep breath, but I didn't feel winded. My muscles ached, of course, a workout ache instead of an injury ache. I was pleasantly surprised with the condition of my knees and my feet.

I felt confident, even knowing what was ahead of me. I had studied books, knew the route, and understood that all the other days combined would not equal what was in store for me in the next eighteen hours. But doubt swirled around, whispering. *You did well, Bob. Even if you don't make it, you got this far. It's about the journey, not the destination. It's great you even attempted this. Not many people you know have tried.* Every statement of encouragement I'd given someone else at some point in my life came back to haunt me, shoving my goal aside. I tried pushing it out of my mind, but it kept springing back like memory foam.

Ernest came for me and I ventured into the freezing cold. The wind buffeted the tents and stirred up clouds of dust. I looked up and saw a snake-like line of twinkling lights along the mountainside. Hikers and their headlamps. They beckoned me, guiding my way. Once we moved out of the protection of the tents, the wind grabbed hold of me. It was an effort to remain upright. The wind came from my right and I could only be glad it wasn't from the front, blowing dust in my face and slowing my progress. The only saving grace was the occasional outcropping giving us relief.

We got into some serious rock scrambling, and with it came protection from the wind. It was still cold, but my exertion kept me warm. The worst part was my hands. I had chosen gloves instead of mitts so I could handle my poles and grasp rocks better, something I would re-think if I were to do this again. My fingers became cold very quickly from grasping my pole straps. It was a choice between using my poles and sticking my hands under my arms. The path in this section was like a series of steps, each one about twice the height of normal stairs. Place your foot on the next step, grab some nearby rock and hoist yourself up. Next step, next step, again and again. I was starting to breathe heavier as we climbed. An hour or two later; it was hard to tell, we broke free from the rocky climbing and took a sharp left. I had a clear line of sight up the slope and saw the zig-zag line of twinkling lights before me.

Now the steep portion began. Every step was deliberate and controlled, with a deep breath in between. I drank from my two water bottles as my camel tubing had frozen. I had been thawing it by blowing back on it to keep it clear, but some time ago Ernest had taken my backpack to lighten my load. The path here was mostly scree and made progress slow. The gravel sat loose, ready to slide down at the lightest of touch. Each step I would slide back a little, even with my poles.

You really are alone on the mountain. Sure, you have your guide and hundreds of people passing you or you passing them, but it's you and the mountain. At first, it's your friend, beckoning you, encouraging you to achieve your goal, filling you with hope and excitement. Then it slowly chips away at you, like a sculptor creating a piece from a block of granite. It breaks you down physically, slowly, just enough to open a small crack. A crack wide enough to insert the wedge of doubt. On summit day it brings out the big hammer to slam down on that wedge, forcing doubt in even deeper. Having taken away any physical reserves you may possess, the mountain then attacks your mind. It talks to you. Mocks you. It's you and the mountain. All alone.

I'm not sure how I made it through the next couple of hours until the sun rose over the Mawazi Peak, but as I paused for a few photos, I was rejuvenated. Daylight brought the promise of better things. Warmer temperatures. A little hope. Some interference for the striking hammer.

Then the trail got steeper.

We were onto some loose, gravelly stones and a slope so steep I could reach forward and touch it. For the next hour, there were switchbacks upon switchbacks, not long, only about twenty feet or so, a constant reminder of the futility of walking hundreds of feet to gain ten in elevation. Back and forth, back and forth. Onward and upward. I was exhausted.

People were now coming down the mountain after achieving their goal. My friend who lent me his phone passed by with words of encouragement. *Push onward. Don't give up.* All the people passing by were like a double-edged sword. I was bolstered by their words of encouragement, but constantly reminded I was hours behind and running out of time.

The next forty-five minutes were the hardest of the climb. The slippery scree and altitude were getting to me, but I persevered. I could now see some people gathered at Stella Point, a resting place at the edge of the crater. It never seemed to get closer. There were no switchbacks now, just energy-sapping loose scree. Two steps forward, one step sliding back. Exhausting and demoralizing.

Stella Point marks a significant point in the climb. If you make it this far, you get a certificate. A silver one, mind you. The one that says you didn't make it all the way. The silver one that says you lost. Lost to the mountain. A participation certificate. Thanks for showing up. Better luck next time.

Stella Point also signifies a turning point in your climb. From here it is less than a kilometre and only 500-foot elevation to get to the top. At 19,000 feet that's still a bugger of a hike but comparatively easier than my last two hours. It's also a quick resting spot.

I took the final few steps and plunked myself down on a rock, absolutely knackered, as the saying goes. I welcomed the rest and snacks. My camel tube had thawed, and I drank lots of energy-drink as I watched the steady stream of hikers coming from the peak. We sat for some time recuperating, Ernest watching me closely. Behind me was the steep grade I had just climbed. In front was a huge crater. Around to my left was the trail leading to the peak. Not that I noticed or cared about any of the views.

I was starting to feel better when I saw the older gentleman with his grandson/son stroll down from the peak, his oxygen bottle in tow.

Flashes of the nuns came back to me.

They congratulated me and said it was just another half an hour. Ernest chuckled and said it was a lot longer than that.

I began to pack my stuff and said I was ready to go. Ernest looked at me.

"No Bob. We will not be able to get down in time. You are too tired. We have to go back, now."

It was the only time during the whole trip, except for introductions, that Ernest called me Bob. I don't think I can properly explain the emotions that flooded through me. Disappointment, feelings of failure, inadequacy, were but a few. I was exhausted, the altitude messing with me. I began to cry, not a weepy, few-tears-down-the-cheek cry, but a sobbing, body-shaking cry. I remember blubbering some stuff to Ernest and eventually getting myself under control.

"I've come all the way from Canada to do this. Don't take this away from me." I pleaded and promised and reluctantly he agreed. He was mumbling to himself and shaking his head as we prepared to leave. At this point, he knew my condition better than I did. *Be careful what you wish for.*

It took all the effort I had to stand. We started on a gentle slope following the trail around the edge of the crater. Ernest was around twenty feet ahead of me, urging a more rapid pace, having given up on *polepole*. I was stiff from sitting, tired, emotional, and oxygen-deprived. All of a sudden, an overwhelming desire to quit came over me. I don't know where it came from, perhaps the wedge of doubt had broken through. My mind was playing tricks, a seesaw of emotions.

You can't do this.

Get your ass going.

You're not good enough.

Come on, suck it up.

I stopped and began to turn around, calling out to Ernest.

"Okay, let's go back."

I froze. What have I done? How could I do this to myself? Even if I change my mind, he won't let me continue now. I began to cry again, this time silent tears washing the grime from my face. An inner sense of dread overcame me, a chill ran through my body. All this for nothing, all the training, hours and hours of hiking, climbing stairs, preparation, all for nothing. I looked up, ready to see Ernest's knowing face. Staring me down. Judging me.

All I saw was his back as he continued to walk up the slope. Either he had not heard me or chose to ignore it, I'll never know. The sight of him walking away inspired me to push forward. I was determined to complete this no matter what. I'm not sure what drove me the last hour up to the peak, whether it was guts, determination, or stubbornness but I'll be forever thankful. I've said I was exhausted before, but I truly did not know the meaning of the word until this last hour. We arrived at the peak at approximately 10:00 AM, four hours behind schedule.

There is no actual peak. There is no gazing down thousands of feet. The highest point in Africa is situated on the edge of a crater. That crater is around 2.5 kilometres wide and between 500-600 feet deep. I am surrounded by a lunar-like landscape, with glaciers; several of them hundreds of feet thick. On top of one is a weather mast. The glaziers are receding, not necessarily from warming, but from a change in the amount of precipitation during the rainy season. I looked around in amazement at the vastness of this mountain. A crow landed near the edge. What's it doing way up here? For some reason this is hilarious, and I start to giggle. Was my mind playing tricks?

Altitude, euphoria, oxygen deprivation, and who knows what else, all contributed to a surreal experience at the top. I had planned an inspirational video up there, but in all honesty, I couldn't do it. Everything was in slow motion and concentrating that long would have been impossible. We got some pictures of us beside the sign as proof of us being there, then we sat and ate some more snacks. A kaleidoscope of images passed before me, my research, training, preparation, and the climb. Along with those came the emotions, the ups and downs, doubt, desire, and stubbornness. I had finally made it after 45 years.

Dreams do come true.

However, dreams come at a price, and I had not yet seen the bill.

***

The Descent

We packed up and left the sign behind. Shortly after that, it all turned into a shit-storm. I guess you could say it went all downhill from there.

As Ernest had suspected I did not have the energy to get down the mountain. Let me rephrase that. I believe I had the energy, but I began having trouble drawing in air. We made it back to Stella Point without incident and continued down with no break. Instead of taking the countless switchbacks, we took a "shortcut" straight down the scree. The idea was to kind of "ski" down, slipping and sliding on the loose gravel for the next 2,000 feet. My knees were not up for it, and I couldn't catch my breath. Ernest had his arm around me trying to drag me along. It was now noontime and we were supposed to be at the camp by now, almost six hours late and with 2,500 feet still to descend.

I could tell Ernest was getting concerned. People would be arriving at the base camp, and we should have been moved by now. The arriving hikers needed our space for their tents. But more important, he was concerned about my condition. My breathing was becoming more forced, and I could only take a dozen steps without stopping.

There were no helicopter evacuations off the mountain when I went. The only way was to be carried down. Around three o'clock two of my porters met us on our descent and the three of them formed a type of chair lift and began carrying me down the mountainside. I was embarrassed but just as disconcerted with my declining health. Breathing became harder as they struggled to get me down.

We arrived at the "steps" part of the descent, and it was too narrow and dangerous for the chair lift. I was on my own, tenderly stepping down uneven "stairs" with bad knees and wobbly legs, huffing and puffing. My feet were sore and blistering from the descent, and my toes were numb. I could not lower myself with my right leg anymore, so my left was doing all the work. Down, down, down, an endless series of unrelenting descent, until finally, it began to level out. I was able to walk again; well as normal as my jelly legs would allow.

Base camp came into view around 6 pm, six hours after I should have been there. I made it to my tent and flopped down on my cot. Ernest said I could have a quick soup and we would need to continue to the next camp, so pack up my extra stuff. I removed my boots and noticed the ends of my socks were blood-soaked. Carefully I removed them, tearing a bit of skin. The ends of several toes were bloody and mangled from sliding forward against my boots during the descent. I got out my 2nd Skin and tried applying some but could not do it. My legs were so stiff I couldn't bring them up onto my knee so I could reach my feet, and I couldn't bend over because I was huffing and puffing so badly. As a matter of fact, I was having trouble breathing sitting down and needed to stand.

I was puffing like a steam engine when a porter brought my soup. I asked if Ernest could come and put the 2nd Skin on my feet. I tried eating the soup, but it was almost impossible. At this point I was sucking in air constantly, those deep breaths you take before you dive underwater. My breathing rate was close to forty per minute. I would take one spoonful of soup, swallow it, then take ten to fifteen breaths before I caught my wind enough to try another spoonful.

Ernest came by and fixed my feet, while I stood on one leg, eating my soup. Except for the seriousness of the situation, it might have been comical. There were no crews nearby that had any oxygen. He packed my extra gear away for the porters and went to give them instructions. *Pack up, race to the next camp, set up, and hurry back to help get me down.* The best first aid for me was descending. We headed off down the path to the next camp some seven kilometers away. I had been up for nineteen hours now and had burned 14,000+ calories. Only six or seven hours to go.

We made slow progress as I needed to stop often to catch my breath. It was getting better as I didn't need to puff as much to maintain airflow, but with a little exertion, I was still short-winded. An hour after we left, the porters went whizzing by, fully loaded, with calls of encouragement and of course, *Babu.*

Two or three hours later I saw lights along the path coming toward us. Ernest said the something-or-other was coming. I can't recall what he said now, but at the time I thought he meant a doctor. No, it was not a doctor. The porters had brought some wheelbarrow contraption to drag me down the mountain. It was a metal-framed stretcher mounted on top of a fat bicycle wheel with shocks. There is an end piece at the base where you place your feet, so you don't slide off. The reason for that became apparent soon enough. There were handles on the front, back, and sides, enough for six to stabilize it. They asked me to climb in and lay down. My sleeping bag fit under my head for some comfort. Then they began to strap me in, around my shins, thighs, waist, and chest, so I wouldn't fly out. Wait, what? Fly out? A little concern overcame me as I visualized the upcoming rocky trail. It would be okay; they would take their time. I couldn't deal with the strap around my chest, so they left that undone and I was able to free my arms, much to my relief. I was doing okay laying on a 45-degree angle, but when they lifted the front and leveled me out my breathing became harder. In one minute, that was forgotten, as a new fear overcame me. I was sure we were about to crash.

They took off like fresh stallions in a chariot race. These skinny little porters could run like the wind, aided by the downhill gradient. I likened it to a controlled crash landing. I'm sure they hit every rock and bump on that trail and would bet money someone was throwing extra rocks under that tire. I was vibrating like an off-centered washing machine on the spin cycle. There were a couple of cliffs they had to lower me down. I volunteered to get out -- demanded it actually -- but they said no, it was no problem. Although I did not understand what they were saying, I read the anxiety in their voices as they lowered me. The brakeman's feet skidded, and he screamed louder as my chariot gained momentum over the cliff. There is nothing more disconcerting than being strapped down, unable to move, as you get lowered over a cliff. I envisioned myself falling, flipping over face-first onto the rocky ground. My respect for the porters tripled during my ride down the mountain face.

I'm not sure exactly what I encountered medically on the mountain. My wife, and some of her nursing colleagues, reasoned afterward that I had a mucous plug and some fluid on the lungs. Whatever it was, the ride assisted me greatly in overcoming it. It was like chest therapy with the continual thumping of the rocky path. An hour into my wheelbarrow ride I began coughing and asked them to stop. I got unstrapped and horked out some incredible produce. I coughed and gagged and threw up for about fifteen minutes. What looked like a huge jellyfish lay on the side of the trail. I returned to my chariot feeling much better. I had to stop twice more to clear my lungs, and with each expulsion felt better.

We arrived at the camp around 2:30 in the morning 27 hours after I woke up to begin my ascent of Kili. One of the wardens had a good look at me. I'm not sure what qualifications he had other than years of experience, but between him and Ernest, I was declared recovered enough that I did not need to continue my descent that night. My breathing had improved but I was still puffing when I took short walks. I ate another bowl of soup and settled into a bed in the ranger station. It took a long time for me to be able to lay down and relax. I felt like I couldn't get any air and bolted up to a sitting position numerous times before exhaustion overcame me and I fell asleep around four in the morning.

Seven o'clock came early. I ate a quick breakfast and steeled myself for another adventure with my chariot. Eleven kilometers and roughly a 6000 ft descent. Fresh stallions hitched to my chariot and away we charged. I preferred the darkness of the previous night over the nightmare of details flashing before me in the daylight. Every obstacle was clearly seen. As we descended from the moorlands into the alpine forest, tree roots replaced rocks. Rock ledges became wooden stairs. Narrower trails meant the porters on the side handles often had to let go to get themselves around trees. This caused the wheelbarrow to tilt awkwardly and my heart rate to increase. The option to slow down was not thought of or ignored. Twice they lost control and we spun out, the litter on its side.

At one point during a flat area of the trail, I managed to fall asleep; don't ask me how. I woke up to lush forests and a smooth trail. Another hour and we arrived at a road. An "ambulance" was waiting (really, just a jeep) to transport me the rest of the way. I dismounted from my chariot, a little unsteady.

At this point, I realized I had made it. I was alive and had accomplished my goal.

I graciously tipped my rescue crew. Three of them were my porters. I briefly wondered how their kit and the equipment they normally carried were getting down the mountain. Did they bring it down last night? Were the remaining porters doubling up on their loads? I never did find out as my mind turned to other things.

I got into the jeep and rode for another fifteen minutes to several buildings similar to the starting gate. I thought I would be seeing some sort of doctor, but it didn't happen. Ernest showed up and we reported to the ranger station, and I received my certificate, a gold one, proclaiming that on October 14th, 2016 at 10:00 am I had climbed to the highest point in Africa.

My porters were all gathered together, and they did a victory dance for me. Then Ernest asked to give a short speech. This was unexpected and I began to choke up trying to explain what this meant to me. I thanked them numerous times for literally saving my life and this was reflected when I tripled their tips. They did another dance, and then we headed to the van.

On the drive back to the hotel I reflected on the last eight days. The excitement and thrill of my first day. My tiredness and emotional turmoil throughout the trip. Fatigue and doubt. I remembered in detail the final ascent. The long grueling hours, step after step, hour after hour. I remembered my rollercoaster ride of emotions. My euphoria of reaching the peak. The beginnings of my troubles. Would I get off the mountain alive? My descent.

As we rounded the last corner to the motel, the mountain came into view outside my window. It loomed over me, even from that distance, mocking me, beckoning me. We were all alone again, just the two of us, even with the full van. It whispered to me.

Careful what you wish for!

You can see pictures of my accent at: http://www.waywardwanderers.ca/kilimanjaro/

About the Author

Bob Nothnagel served 25 years in the Canadian Armed Forces. He lives in Hamilton Ontario with his wife, Teresa. They enjoy travelling as well as the outdoors, hiking, and kayaking. When not writing, Bob spends time with his grandchildren, where they go on many adventures.

Manufactured by Amazon.ca
Bolton, ON